MURDER AT EIGHT!

The setting, one newsman wrote, was "almost unreal, almost like something out of Dashiell Hammett or Rex Stout."

It was just a little after eight P.M. in a flat on Beekman Hill, the muted façade of Manhattan wealth and glamour. In a hundred other flats in these quiet, clean streets, they were finishing the third Martini and thinking about eating.

In Number 313, the detectives from the East 51st Street station found their handmaiden—violent death. Only the trappings were more exotic than usual.

They found Patricia Burton Lonergan, who had been twenty-two. The seven million dollars she would someday inherit no longer mattered.

She lay flung across the huge Second Empire four-poster bed. She was nude, and her arms were folded up around her face as if she were warding off a blow. The silk bedspread beneath her was heavily stained with blood. On the bed next to her was a fourteen-inch brass candlestick, its glass inlay shattered and the whole of it covered with blood.

The room was a scene of rumpled violence. Patsy Burton Lonergan had fought for her life. Human flesh was found under her fingernails.

It would not soon be forgotten, what happened in this room, by Patsy Lonergan's avenger —the state of New York, which fought to take the life of Wayne Thomas Lonergan, husband of the beautiful and dead society girl.

THE GIRL IN
MURDER FLAT

A Gold Medal Original
by

Mel Heimer

WILDSIDE PRESS

THE GIRL IN
MURDER FLAT

Chapter One

THE SETTING, one newsman wrote, was "almost unreal, almost like something out of Dashiell Hammett or Rex Stout."

It was an apartment in Beekman Hill, the last residential refuge of glamour and wealth in Manhattan. In a hundred other apartments in these quiet, clean streets, a hundred men in dinner jackets and women in dinner gowns were finishing the third Martini and thinking about eating. It was just a little after eight P.M.

The detectives from the East 51st Street station hadn't had too far to go—just to number 313, down the block. As they entered the apartment house, they knew what they would see when they reached the luxurious bedroom. The hasty phone call had told them that. They would see their handmaiden, violent death. Only the trappings would be more exotic than usual, and much more incongruous.

They expected to see four live ones and a dead one, and they did.

The live ones were an elderly nurse named Elizabeth Black, dazed but efficient; a chic, middle-aged woman with upswept gray hair named Lucille Burton Wolfe; a husky, good-looking captain of the United States Marines named Peter Elser, who in other days had helped deliver a different kind of violence to Yale footballers in behalf of Harvard; and a very small boy called Billy, who was asleep.

The dead one was the prettiest of the group. And the bloodiest.

Her name was Patricia Burton Lonergan. She had been twenty-two.

She also had been the sole heiress to seven million dollars. When the men from the East 51st Street station found her in the Beekman Hill apartment, the seven million dollars no longer seemed to matter much.

She sprawled across the huge Second Empire four-poster bed. She was nude and her arms were folded around her face as if she were warding off a blow. The silk bedspread beneath her was heavily stained with blood. Under the bed lay a fourteen-inch brass candlestick, handsomely inlaid with green glass. The candlestick's twin lay on the bed next to the body of Patsy Lonergan. *Its* glass inlay was shattered, and the whole stick was covered with blood.

On a bench near the bed were scattered the components of the New York uniform: mink jacket, black dress, black shoes, and nylons.

The rest of the room was a shambles. Within the rumpled violence of the scene, it first appeared as if the room had been sealed completely. The door had had to be forced, earlier, by Pete Elser, and the Venetian blinds were drawn. A closer inspection disclosed one window partly open, another closed but unlocked, and the third locked but with its catch broken. When the detectives pulled up the blinds, they looked out on a fire escape fashioned in the form of a balcony, which ran to within a few feet of a balcony on an adjoining building. Below was a well-kept garden.

On this Sunday in October of 1943, General Sir Bernard L. Montgomery told the British Eighth Army that the end of the Second World War was in sight. The Brooklyn Dodgers rehired Leo Durocher as manager. American troops drove three miles up the road to Rome, and in New Rochelle, New York, residents reported the first snow of winter, only to be told by the weather bureau it was too warm to snow. And in a Manhattan court proceeding, racketeer Frank Costello blandly said that his word carried more weight with Tammany Hall than President Roosevelt's.

In Beekman Hill, the men from Homicide and from the East 51st Street station, faced with a gory tableau, took off their hats, loosened their collars, and got down to work.

By midnight they had arrested the last man known to have seen Patsy Burton alive.

By dawn their coworkers in Toronto, Canada, had picked up twenty-six-year-old Royal Canadian Air Force cadet Wayne Thomas Lonergan for questioning. He was Patsy Lonergan's husband, and he had two prominent gashes on his chin.

The boys from Homicide were on familiar ground. There was nothing new to them about murder on Beekman Hill.

They remembered the Nancy Titterton and the Veronica Gedeon cases, and at least one of them might have said something about these things coming in threes. For Nancy and Veronica, like Patsy, had been beautiful young New York women.

Nancy Titterton was found raped and strangled with her pajamas on Good Friday, 1936, in her apartment at 22 Beekman Place—just around the corner from Patsy Burton's home. Less than a year later, an upholsterer's assistant named John Fiorenza, who had a record as a sex offender, died in the electric chair for the murder.

A year after the Titterton case, police discovered the

bodies of lovely artists' model Veronica Gedeon, her mother, and a male boarder in the Gedeons' home at 316 East 50th Street, almost directly adjoining the Lonergan residence-to-be. The women had been strangled and the man ice-picked to death. In November 1938, sculptor Robert Irwin was sentenced to 139 years in prison for the three killings. A month after the sentencing, he was declared insane. Police remembered that case particularly because Irwin had sought emasculation, claiming his passion interfered with his career.

Pete Elser, who was scheduled to have dinner with Patricia Lonergan on that threatening, raw October night, came over to the Beekman Hill apartment early. He came at the suggestion of Lucille Burton Wolfe, who said worriedly that her daughter Patsy hadn't been seen all day. When Elser broke down the bedroom door, he found the remains of a girl who, just three months before, had been told by the law that she and she alone eventually would receive the seven million dollars left in trust by Max E. Bernheimer, the brewer who was her late grandfather.

Her father, William Burton, had died not long before. It was because of his death, trustee Alfred Rose disclosed, "that we asked the Surrogate to make a construction of the estate and determine the heir under terms of Mr. Bernheimer's will." The New York County Surrogate Court ruled that on the death of Patricia's grandmother, Mrs. Frederick Housman—who had remarried after Max Bernheimer's death—the millions would become Patricia's. Under this court construction, which followed the line of direct family succession, the fortune eventually would (in the far distant likelihood of Patsy Burton's death) go to Wayne Lonergan—the Wayne Lonergan who was one and one-half years old, not the Wayne Lonergan who was twenty-six.

There was nothing new about sudden death in the Burton, or Bernheimer, family.

The brewery was founded in the mid 1800's by Emanuel Bernheimer, but it had flowered under the guidance of his sons, Simon and Max, who, in 1903, bought out the John F. Betz plant in uptown Manhattan, then described as "the world's largest brewery, with an artesian well of almost limitless capacity, which furnishes the purest water." Ultimately, the firm became known as the Bernheimer and Schwartz Pilsner Brewing Company, with Anton Schwartz, a partner, being the man credited with introducing the manufacture of Pilsner beer to the East.

Simon Bernheimer died while playing the bass drum in the Mecca Temple of the Mystic Shrine. Max Bernheimer, who in his fifty-eight years had become a philanthropist and art lover (he left the Metropolitan Museum of Art a $250,000 stamp collection said to rival King Edward's), dropped dead of a heart attack in Supreme Court, Brooklyn, after testifying in a $10,000 suit brought against the brewery by a former employee.

The wealthy and socially prominent Bernheimers, true to tabloid expectations, had chalked up one or two peccadilloes along the way.

In 1907, Mrs. Max Bernheimer, later Mrs. Frederick Housman and executrix of the trust fund, broke elegantly into page one of almost every New York newspaper by holding a dinner at which the guests sat on the tables, ate from the chairs, began their meal with coffee and nuts, and ended it with soup and oysters. And just a month before this, George Bernheimer—Patsy Burton's uncle—celebrated his coming of age, according to newspaper reports, "by turning a room at Delmonico's into an oasis. It was supposed to be a stag party of 100 but after a while there came two dozen or so chorus girls to liven things up."

It was Patsy's father, William, that changed the name from Bernheimer to Burton. He died three years before the murder on Beekman Hill.

When friends of Patsy tried to recall her, after her death, their stories conflicted sharply. Some said she was a party girl, wild and ready for anything; others said she was sensitive, loyal, and confused by the café-society atmosphere in which she grew up.

If there was sensitivity to Patsy, it might have come from Bill Burton, who was a portrait painter and a good one. He once even painted Mussolini from life. According to Lucille Wolfe Burton, he had other traits that often are attributed to artists. When she divorced him in 1926, five years after Patsy's birth, she charged that he had hurled a suitcase at her in a rage, thrown her downstairs, knocked her down, and used profane language at various times.

But Bill and Lucille Burton weren't through with each other. Four years after the divorce, they remarried.

"We worshiped the child," the striking Mrs. Burton said of this unusual event. "She was the main reason why we remarried."

Patsy Burton was born in Long Branch, New Jersey, on September 1, 1921, twenty-two years and fifty-three days before a brass candlestick was used to beat her to death.

Rumor had it that she grew up in an atmosphere of decadence. More than any of the other things said about her daughter, this infuriated Lucille Burton.

"How could Patsy lead a decadent life," she exclaimed bitterly, "when she was reared in a cloistered life just as any well-born French child would be, in the most conservative schools?" Her husband, she added, never allowed the adolescent Patsy to come to their parties, bob her hair, varnish her nails, wear rouge or lipstick. "If anything," she said, "Mr. Burton and I were too strict with her."

The French education came about early; the Burtons went abroad when Patsy was a couple of weeks old and remained in Paris for five years, or until their divorce. Patsy then lived with Lucille for four years, after which came the remarriage. The family then lived in Cannes from 1930 to 1939. Until she was four, she always had a nurse; after that there were governesses. There was a Miss Wilmott and a Mlle. Aimone. It was Mlle. Aimone that came to Mrs. Burton after the murder and said she would testify for Patsy's character if she could. And Miss Wilmott, who stayed with the Burtons until Patsy was seventeen, received a big Christmas box in England days after the slaying—from Patsy Burton Lonergan.

The Burton house in Cannes was turned into a hospital in the late thirties, and Lucille took charge of the Canteen Militaire in Cannes. Patsy and Bill left for America in 1939, chiefly because he had a weak heart, but Patsy's mother stayed on until after the fall of France.

The New York World's Fair, a sprawling, raucous carnival strewn across the marshes of Flushing Meadows, was opened in 1939 and held over for another year. It was there, most reports have it, that Bill Burton met a big, good-looking Canadian boy named Wayne Lonergan, whose job was pushing a ricksha.

Bill Burton's heart gave out in October of 1940. From then until December, when her mother got back to America, Patsy reportedly lived at 1000 Park Avenue with a chaperon. And when Mrs. Burton returned from overseas, "she met me at the boat and went immediately to my hotel. I only speak of this to show how carefully she was watched over."

In the months before her father died, Patsy Burton saw a good deal of Wayne Lonergan, who must have injected an incongruous note into her carefully ordered existence. His parents, Mr. and Mrs. Thomas Lonergan, never had any money. Wayne went to St. Michael's College in his native Toronto, and later to Toronto Business College, but he never had any money, either. In 1935 he was a special constable for the provincial police department, later he worked for the International Nickel Company, and still later he was a lifeguard.

There was no particular pattern to his early working life—but after he met Bill Burton at the World's Fair, one seemed to shape up.

"I thought him completely selfish," Patsy's mother told reporters, "and totally heartless—but Patsy didn't agree. She had fallen in love."

It was a head-on collision between the glib, easy-going Lonergan and the chic, protective Mrs. Burton. Wayne called at their hotel to offer his sympathy on her husband's death. Patsy's mother responded by taking her daughter to California, in the hope that she would forget the "completely selfish" man. But Patsy, infatuated, did not forget. She and Wayne fled to Las Vegas and were married.

"Of course, I was heartbroken," Mrs. Burton recalled, "but what could I do except stand by Patsy?"

From the very beginning, though, Wayne and Patsy quarreled. Even on their honeymoon, according to friends and relatives, they were at each other constantly, bitterly.

"They fought like cats and dogs," said Reginald Wright, treasurer of a Manhattan greeting-card concern and a friend of the young couple's. "There was never any peace between them. Once, when they got into an argument, I heard her say to Wayne, 'I suppose that's to be expected when a girl marries a man who is beneath her.'"

Wright got them an apartment at one time—the Lonergans lived in several expensive flats during their two years together, more or less as man and wife—and he promptly got complaints from the neighbors, asking that he "try to get them out."

"They used to say that her screams were unbearable," Wright said. "They said she used to scream she was being murdered."

Wright told Wayne of the complaints, but Lonergan shrugged them off. "Oh, we had a row and I beat her up," he said jokingly, according to Wright. Patsy used to call Wayne a "heel," and he "had a few choice words for her, too," Wright recalled.

While they lived together, Wayne and Patsy saw her mother nearly every day. "I introduced Wayne to my friends until his attitude became unbearable," said Mrs. Burton, "and then I told Patsy I couldn't have him come to my home any more. What forced that decision? His lies. His boasting. He couldn't tell the truth if his life depended on it."

In some quarters, the tale was that Patsy bought herself endless quantities of expensive clothes. "She never bought herself one decent thing until she and Wayne were separated," Mrs. Burton protested. "She lavished everything on him. He didn't have a cent of his own. She wasn't lazy; she worked hard—nurses' aide, first aid, the blood bank, Bellevue and St. Clare's Hospital."

The tale was, too, that Patsy and Lucille had drifted away from each other. To answer that one, Mrs. Burton made public a note. "Darling Doodles," it read, "I am very fortunate to have you as a mother. I love you very much. These are the first tulips of the season. Mouse."

"Patsy called me Doodles; I called her Mouse," Mrs. Burton said. "She was always bringing me little presents."

Whatever Patsy was really like, this much seemed certain: After two years of stormy life together, the Lonergans seemed headed for divorce.

At first, according to her mother, Patsy thought it would be just a separation. Then she decided to make the split legal and final. "Wayne tried to fight it," Lucille said, "first by attempting to enlist in the U.S. Army, then the Canadian Air Force."

Legal records bear out her claim.

Six months before the slaying, young Billy Lonergan's mother made hasty arrangements to ensure that the seven-million-dollar fortune would go eventually to her son. On August 21, 1943, Surrogate James A. Foley in New York decreed in effect that the child was next in line to the millions. There was an ironic note to the proceedings. Attorney John G. Saxe, appearing as special guardian for the child, petitioned to have affairs so arranged that in the event of the death of Stella Housman, Max Bernheimer's remarried widow, Patsy would inherit the estate if she was living. If Patsy were not alive, her son would be the heir at Stella Housman's death. The prospect of Patsy being dead at such a time, unlikely as it seemed, moved Saxe to say: "That would be a great misfortune for him."

Those were the important parts of Patsy Burton's life, and the lives before hers, that shaped her destiny until that week end of tragedy in October 1943. When the week end was done, her part in the drama was over. For the others, it had hardly begun.

Chapter Two

THE POLICE OF NEW YORK CITY move swiftly, if not
always skillfully. When Pete Elser broke in the door of
Patsy Lonergan's bedroom, the fuse was lighted, the chain
reaction began.

An assistant medical examiner, called to the scene,
placed the time of death at about ten A.M. Sunday. Patsy
had died after a wild battle, as evidenced by the violently disarranged room, the bloodstains on the carpeting,
and the blood smeared along the walls of the stairway
that led from the first-floor stoop to the bedroom. Human
flesh was found under Patsy's fingernails.

Then came the arrests.

The first was that of Mario Gabellini, an Italian-born,
forty-year-old interior decorator. He was detained as a
material witness. He had brought Patsy Lonergan back
to her apartment at about six A.M. Sunday, according to
his story. Homicide men questioned him for more than
twelve hours, during which he said that he had known
Patsy "for some time," and "was out with her all Saturday night." Brought before General Sessions Judge Jonah
J. Goldstein on Monday afternoon, he was ordered held
in $10,000 bail.

Detectives next headed for the East 79th Street apartment of a good-looking blonde bit actress named Jean
Murphy, known also as Jean Jaburg. She was Mario
Gabellini's counterpart; if he was the last one known to
have seen Patsy Lonergan alive, Jean Murphy was the
last person known to have seen Wayne Lonergan before
the killing. She had dated him that Saturday night, and
had left him, she said, at three A.M. Sunday, when he told
her that he was going to the apartment of a friend in the
same building in which she lived to sleep.

"It's such a sordid thing," she told reporters when
the police were through with their preliminary question-

14

ing. "I don't want to be mixed up in it." Under further probing, she said that she had been introduced to Lonergan by John Harjes, a handsome banking-firm heir who, it developed, leased the apartment in which Lonergan said he had gone to sleep.

That introduction, she added, had come just the day of the date. Harjes said his friend was in town on leave from Canada and had tickets for *One Touch of Venus,* the Mary Martin show. With another girl, they went to the theatre, then to Twenty-One, and finally the Blue Angel, a smart supper club, after which Lonergan took her home. "Mr. Lonergan acted the perfect gentleman all the time," Jean Murphy said. "All of Mr. Harjes' friends I have met have been perfect gentlemen."

Lonergan phoned her Sunday around one P.M. and asked her to have lunch. They went to the Plaza, where, she declared, his attitude was "perfectly normal" and "nonchalant." Newsmen told her that Lonergan, picked up in Toronto by police, reportedly had scratches on his face. She said she hadn't noticed any on Sunday.

"Miss" Murphy, it developed, was not quite correct. A one-time movie bit player who had appeared in the last edition of *George White's Scandals,* she was still married to her second husband, Hugo Jaburg, president of the R. C. Williams Company, distributors of the Royal Scarlet brand of foods, but had been separated from him for a year and a half.

A magazine publisher named Tom Farrell added another tile to the mosaic. He told of Patsy Burton's last Saturday night on earth.

Farrell had dined that night at Louise's, a smart French restaurant on East 58th Street, with model Jean Goodman and realty broker Bob Dasy. Gabellini and Patsy joined them. Patsy ate a hearty meal; hors d'oeuvres, broiled lamb chops, and black coffee. She looked, Farrell said, "remarkably well." Death must have been the farthest thing from her mind.

"It was Saturday night and she was out for a good time," Farrell said. "She talked and laughed and danced as if she didn't have a care in the world. She even discussed her husband without bitterness or sorrow. I think she enjoyed herself more than anyone else in our party." She "certainly wasn't worrying about anything," he added, although she said she had seen Lonergan that afternoon when he arrived from Toronto to visit her and little Billy.

Farrell and Miss Goodman first met Patsy one week end at Yorktown Heights, New York, introduced by Gabellini, whom Farrell said he had known for five years. Later they dined at Patsy's apartment one night, and Farrell remembered that dinner as "charming." "She had an intelligent, matter-of-fact approach to life," he said. "She was well educated, spoke French like a native, and impressed me as an altogether sane person."

It was at the dinner in Louise's, he said, that someone suggested going to the Stork Club to dance. "We're likely to bump into my husband," Patsy said. "Let's go to El Morocco instead." Farrell said she talked freely about her separation from Wayne. In the end the party went to the Stork Club after all, and didn't run into Lonergan.

Two of the topics that night in Louise's stayed in Farrell's memory. Patsy joined animatedly in discussing both. One was the Russian victories in the Second World War, then raging; the other was Sir Harry Oakes, the baronet of the Bahamas, who had been murdered three and a half months before.

Farrell told police that the party adjourned to his midtown hotel room after leaving the Stork, and stayed until six A.M. He was certain of the time. His watch had stopped and he checked with the hotel desk to find out the hour. Then, he said, Mario Gabellini took Patsy home.

To some it seemed as if every cop in New York had been assigned to the murder investigation. Actually, the working force was relatively small; sixty detectives under the direction of Acting Deputy Chief Inspector Patrick Kenny and Assistant District Attorney John F. Loehr.

In the first few hours they discovered this:

1. Two diaries and an address book were found in the murder room. They contained between two and three hundred names and addresses, some of them cafés, ga-

rages, and restaurants, many merely names of men. The diaries weren't much help. They consisted mostly of appointments. One was for two-thirty P.M. Saturday for "cocktails, Mario, Lexington Ave. apartment."

2. The superintendent of the Lexington Avenue apartment house where Gabellini had had a flat until a month before the slaying said the decorator had been threatened with dispossession many times during his several years there. And at the apartment house across the street, where Gabellini now lived, neighbors said they hadn't heard any sounds in his flat during the month he had been there—until Sunday of the murder week end, when their quiet afternoon was disturbed by hammering.

3. Chester Burt Fentress, a singer who owned the building where the Lonergans lived, said they had leased their apartment on September 15, moving from 938 Park Avenue. They drove up in a large car, showed good bank references, and entertained "lavishly" after moving in, Fentress said.

4. Elizabeth Black, the governess, who slept in a room across the hall from Patsy, said she saw Mrs. Lonergan last on Saturday about seven P.M. She heard no noises of a struggle that night. And, the sixty-year-old nurse added, she hadn't tried to enter Patsy's bedroom all Sunday because her mistress often slept late and didn't come downstairs until evening. Elser, the Marine captain (and son of Max Elser, the horse-show official and ad man, was the first caller, after being summoned by Lucille Burton.

5. The superintendent at 983 Park Avenue, where the Lonergans formerly lived, said they paid $300 monthly for their apartment. Lonergan, apparently, didn't work, and he and Patsy seldom were in the building at the same time. The doorman recalled two frequent visitors—Gabellini and a British army officer, neither of whom was ever there when Lonergan was. Gabellini frequently drove Mrs. Lonergan's Plymouth coupé. A month before the couple moved to Beekman Hill, the English officer's visits ended.

6. It was learned that in August Lonergan had offered for sale, through newspaper classified ad columns, an expensive camera and other photographic equipment. He

gave the address of the Bruehl color photography studios, 480 Lexington Avenue—an address, other photographers in the building said, at which Mario Gabellini had made sets for several photo studios.

7. Patsy Burton's death, Assistant Medical Examiner Milton Helpern's autopsy report read, was caused by "asphyxia by strangulation, together with lacerations of the scalp, possible fracture of the skull, and concussion of the brain."

Up in Toronto, Canadian police held Wayne Lonergan in custody.

He was as calm as any suspect or witness they ever had dealt with, and their questions left him unmoved. He was an RCAF cadet, but when they picked him up he wore civilian clothes. What about that? Lonergan lighted a cigarette and told them that he had been in New York on leave over the week end, and that his uniform had been stolen.

Assistant District Attorney Loehr, flying to Toronto, where later he was joined by New York Detectives William Prendergast and Nicholas Looram, checked every move made by Lonergan, from the time he returned to Canada, nine-thirty P.M. Sunday, until he was picked up Monday at eight-thirty A.M. for questioning. On Monday night, Canadian newsmen asked Lonergan if he denied any connection with his wife's murder. He calmly answered, "Yes." Tuesday morning, as Lonergan was being led from one Toronto station house to another, a reporter called to him, asking if he still maintained his innocence. This time he was not so calm.

"I certainly do!" he shouted back.

The story being pieced together by Canadian and New York authorities began to trickle back to Manhattan, but there was something makeshift about it. There was a report that Lonergan had said he was scratched during a struggle with an American soldier whom he had taken to the Harjes apartment early Sunday. There was a report that Lonergan had claimed the soldier had stolen a hundred dollars and his service uniform from him.

But back in New York, authorities had in their possession a note Lonergan allegedly had left for Harjes on Sunday, thanking the banking heir for the use of the apartment
and commenting that his RCAF clothes had been lost in
an accident. No mention had been made of a struggle or
of a theft.

The man that believed the story least was one who
came into the case a short while after it broke. His name
was Jacob Grumet, and Wayne Lonergan was to see a
lot of him.

Grumet, a thin, mustachioed man later named fire
commissioner of New York City, was attached to the
Homicide Bureau as an assistant district attorney. He
went over to the East 51st Street station to confer with
Inspector Kenny, and when he had heard everything, he
called in the newsmen.

"Personally," Grumet said dourly, "I believe the story
he (Lonergan) has been telling is a cock-and-bull story.
It is fantastic. There is no reason why an American soldier should want a Canadian uniform." Grumet paused
thoughtfully. "Right now," he added, "we are anxious
to have Lonergan here in our jurisdiction."

He got his wish. Lonergan willingly waived extradition
from Toronto to New York.

"I had nothing to do with Pat's murder—absolutely
nothing," he insisted. "I want to be at her funeral and
I want to see our baby. I'm going back to New York to
help the authorities." Together with the two Manhattan
detectives, he boarded a train for New York Tuesday
night. Before the train pulled out, he seemed to have lost
none of his aplomb, talking quietly with Mr. and Mrs.
Joseph Lonergan, an uncle and aunt, and Mrs. June
Cummins, a sister.

Red tape held up Lonergan's arrival in New York. At
Fort Erie, Ontario, on the Canadian border, customs officials stopped the party because Wayne didn't have a
money declaration form. After a delay of an hour and
a half, they resumed the journey and reached Buffalo,
where American immigration authorities immediately took
Lonergan into custody as a nondesirable immigrant. A

three-man board of special inquiry listened briefly to testimony, and then paroled Lonergan in the detectives' care. By that time, no accommodations were available on early-morning trains to New York, so the party spent Tuesday night in Buffalo's Hotel Statler.

While the interrupted journey was in progress, police continued to unearth items. It was learned that Lonergan had been rejected by Army physicians and classified as 4-F when called up for the U.S. draft. A package was found in Harjes' apartment containing face and bath towels that bore reddish stains. Detectives said the stains didn't necessarily have to be blood, and probably were lipstick.

Wayne Lonergan did not get to see his wife buried. Tuesday, while a rainstorm swept through the canyons of New York, about twenty persons attended a service held in Campbell's Funeral Chapel, in which Psalm 91 and an excerpt from John Greenleaf Whittier's *"Snowbound"* were read. Then the remains of Patsy Burton were placed in the ground in Salem Field Cemetery in Brooklyn.

Not long after Lonergan arrived at La Guardia Airport, and detectives herded him through a crowd of onlookers. He was hatless and without a topcoat and his crew cut made him look like a star halfback for some Middle West college. One woman shook her head in astonishment at the sight of him. "Why, he's only a *boy!*" she exclaimed.

"What are you gonna tell 'em, Wayne?" someone in the crowd called out to the prisoner. He turned briefly, but did not answer.

They took him to the district attorney's office, and it turned out that he had a great deal to tell them.

He told them of his sexual aberrations.

Chapter Three

FEW ALIBIS have been so degrading as the one offered
by Wayne Lonergan—and few, at least for a while, have
been so convincing.

Brought directly from the airport to the district attorney's office, Lonergan was questioned for more than
twenty-two hours. Throughout most of it, the big, boyish-
looking air cadet talked freely and almost impassively,
but chain-smoked steadily. Here and there discrepancies
cropped up in his story, but they were minor. When they
were called to his attention, he merely smiled or shrugged
—or lighted another cigarette.

The news from Canada, during Lonergan's interrogation by the police there, had hinted at "unprintable"
testimony. This same testimony initiated the erotic elements
of the case a few hours after the suspect's arrival in New
York. It was revealed that the district attorney's office
had announced flatly that Lonergan said he had been put
in Class 4-F in the draft because he was a homosexual.

"A guilty man, I imagine, would not have offered us
an alibi as degrading as this one," Detective Arthur Harris of Canada had said up in Toronto. And bit by bit,
the alibi came out.

New York police had, roughly, accounted for most of
Lonergan's movements during that week end in town, except for the hours between three and ten A.M. Queried
about this hiatus, he replied, with what seemed to be
candor, with the story of Murray Worcester, the story
that had been hinted at in Canada.

After he took Jean Murphy Jaburg home from their
round of cafés, Lonergan said, he met a soldier while he
was waiting for a cab. The soldier's name was Murray
Worcester, and he accompanied Lonergan to the Harjes
apartment about five A.M., "and we retired."

The events of the next hour and a half were discussed

frankly by Wayne Thomas Lonergan, but the district attorney finally set up a line of delicacy, and did not disclose exactly what they were. It *was* announced that the suspect had claimed the events culminated in a bitter quarrel, with Murray Worcester raking Lonergan's cheek and chin with nails, after which Lonergan fell asleep. He awoke at ten A.M. to find the soldier gone, along with his uniform and his hundred dollars.

Grumet, to whom this story was "fantastic," tried everything in the book—the interrogation at times took on the aspect of an old Edward G. Robinson movie—without much success. His trump card was to bring every important figure in the case face to face with Lonergan during the night. These included Mrs. Jaburg, Harjes, Farrell, Jean Goodman, and Emil Petters, who was Harjes' butler and who already had said that Lonergan *had* slept in the Harjes apartment early Sunday and that he, Petters, had served him breakfast.

"He has admitted nothing," the weary Grumet said at six-ten A.M. on Thursday, as he left his office for his home and a few hours' sleep. Lonergan lay down for a nap on a cot in the D.A.'s office.

While the questioning had gone on, fifty detectives had remained near the D.A.'s quarters to check on the factual replies by the suspect. They unearthed nothing damning to Lonergan. It remained for Maurice B. Worcester, a former Army private who was working in a Bridgeport, Connecticut, war plant, to tear the first small hole in the Lonergan story.

Worcester, a tall, dapper man of forty-four, armed with an honorable discharge from the Army, appeared at the D.A.'s office early Thursday "to clear my name because I have seen stories about Wayne Lonergan and a Murray Worcester."

"I am greatly mystified how Lonergan got my name," Worcester said, "because I do not believe there is another such name in the United States. I don't think that Lonergan picked my name out of the air. I don't know where he got it. I'm no notoriety seeker and I only want my name cleared for the sake of my children."

While Worcester sat in the district attorney's office, Lonergan was brought in briefly. Lonergan was asked if he knew the man. He did not answer.

A little while later, Lonergan was told he had faced and not recognized Murray Worcester.

It was hardly any time at all, after that, before Wayne Thomas Lonergan sighed, stubbed out a lighted cigarette, and said he was ready to tell the story of how he had murdered Patsy Burton Lonergan.

The confession took three hours to tell, and while its text was not announced immediately by police, District Attorney Frank S. Hogan said it went something like this:

Lonergan went to his wife's apartment about eight-forty A.M., a few hours after his date with Jean Murphy Jaburg. Patsy Lonergan had been lying nude on the bedspread, and after she got up and let him in, she returned and threw herself wearily down on the massive bed. He looked at her delicate, pale body, and the dark hair around her cheeks, and then he said:

"I understand you're the belle of El Morocco."

She glared back at him. "I understand *your* behavior hasn't been so good," she replied—and the quarrel had begun. Midway through it, Lonergan asked about the baby. She told him Billy was asleep, and not to go into his room. "Why don't you have lunch with me?" she said, and when he didn't answer, she added, "I'm amazed—I don't seem to be able to control my men any more."

She lay there shaking her head pensively. Then she looked up. "And you're not going to see the baby again," she added.

That did it.

Lonergan had started to pick up his service cap, to leave. Instead he grabbed one of the big candlesticks, wheeled around, and slashed for Patsy's head with it. Dazed and bleeding, she drew herself to a sitting position on the bed, whereupon Lonergan, still blind with rage, reached for the other candlestick and swung that at her, again and again. She clawed at him, her long fingernails raking his chin, but it was no good. She collapsed back across the bed, her blood staining the expensive fabric beneath her, and died.

Lonergan plunged downstairs, smearing the walls and floor of the main stairway with blood, and hurried over to the Harjes apartment. There he took off the bloody uniform, put on one of Harjes' suits, a gray one that fitted loosely, and ordered breakfast from Petters. He stuffed the uniform into a duffel bag, covered his chin wounds with make-up, and took a 79th Street crosstown bus over to the East River.

He had found a dumbbell in Harjes' apartment and had put it into the duffel bag. Now, standing by the East River Drive, he pitched the bag about ten feet out into Hell Gate Channel.

Then he returned to the Harjes flat and phoned Jean Jaburg to ask her for a luncheon date.

The confession done, he took a pen and with a steady hand signed it "Wayne Thomas Lonergan." A detective asked him how he felt. "Well, not so good," he replied. He was asked if he was sorry.

"I don't know whether I did right or not," Lonergan said. Then he paused and looked up. "Yes, I'm sorry," he said. "I'm definitely sorry about it all."

After confessing, he was taken to the East 51st Street station for booking. He still seemed calm, almost indifferent. As the desk sergeant asked the routine questions, he answered almost mechanically. Only one halted him, temporarily. The sergeant asked him his marital status. Lonergan stared, then half turned to Detective Prendergast. The detective leaned over his shoulder, toward the sergeant. "Widower," he said.

By this time, night had fallen. Lonergan was bundled into a car and taken, at the head of a parade of police and reporters and photographers, to the place near the East River where he said he had thrown into the water the duffel bag with the uniform. Still hatless and boyish-looking, he pointed into the channel, striped with the white fingers of the searchlights' glare. Marine launches headed out toward the spot and began grappling. Even as they did so, detectives pushed Lonergan back into a car and took him to Police Headquarters, downtown. He was led into the basement, and finally, stripped of belt, tie, and shoelaces, he was locked into a detention cell at about ten P.M. A cop pushed a chair into position outside the cell door and sat down.

"The big man walked into the little room hesitantly," a newsman wrote, "then sat down on the cot and looked up. A harsh light shone down on him through the grille-work on the ceiling. The unusual face, with its complement of short-cropped Joe-college hair, turned to the light, squinting but unblinking.

"Then, in a little while, Wayne Thomas Lonergan eased himself lengthwise along the cot, let his unlaced shoes drop to the floor, and fell sound asleep. The harrowing week was over."

Chapter Four

MURDER FASCINATES PEOPLE the world over, and in New York its lure seems almost bizarre.

The murder of Patsy Burton Lonergan had everyone in town grabbing for newspapers, on the subway or in the Colony. When Wayne Lonergan was indicted for murder in the first degree—conviction for which means the electric chair in New York—the first phase of the case was settled. For a few weeks, at least, there would be a lull. The city turned back to reading about Field Marshal Montgomery and his drive into Italy from the Adriatic.

Lonergan became a "Main Liner." It was mildly ironic that the young air cadet should be imprisoned in that cell block in New York called the Main Line. He once had traveled in the same social circles as Philadelpha's Main Liners, a somewhat less harmful, and less interesting, species.

Prison officials called him "a cool customer but very polite," who ate and slept well. One item set him apart: He was adamant about not seeing any visitors. An unidentified male friend visited the jail the day after he was locked up, but Lonergan refused to see him. He asked only for cigarettes, for which he paid from the "lot" of Canadian money that prison officials said had been taken from him. He was one of sixty-two homicide prisoners, a third of whom were Main Liners. His cell, on the eighth floor, was eight by six.

The other prisoners accepted him, and he chatted with them agreeably during recreation periods, when they were allowed to walk in the prison quadrangle. A Catholic, he attended mass in the chapel.

The police and the district attorney's office, gathering together the loose ends, went about their business. Reporters pestering Lewis J. Valentine, the tough cop who was New York's police commissioner, were told flatly that

Lonergan would be tried "for first degree or nothing." Later, Wayne was to protest that the D.A.'s office had promised him a deal, in wringing the confession out of him.

In the town's coffee shops and Martini bars, the talk, when it got around to the case, centered on premeditation. Did Lonergan plot the crime, if he were the guilty one, or did he not?

The newspapers went to expert sources. The *World-Telegram* buttonholed James D. C. Murray, a veteran criminal lawyer. He said, "The courts have ruled that the slightest fraction is sufficient lapse of time for premeditation," but he added that he did not see that first-degree murder had been committed, judging from the facts thus far presented.

His point was well taken. There was a new development, however. Dr. Isidore Michel, a midtown physician, had reported to authorities that Lonergan had come to him on the Saturday of the fateful week end, presumably shortly after his flight from Canada, and had asked for a gram of arsenic—"for a friend who wanted to kill himself." Dr. Michel, who refused the request, said Wayne had promised him a hundred dollars if he would agree.

First-degree conviction means finding a man guilty of murder with premeditation, deliberation, and intent to kill.

Second-degree murder is slaying with intent to kill, but without premeditation or deliberation.

Manslaughter, the third charge in the hierarchy, is the killing of a human being without premeditation, deliberation, or intent.

One well-known criminal lawyer had this to say about the first-degree possibilities: "In cases of this character, juries are loath to convict of murder in the first degree. All we know of the facts so far is that he and his wife had a quarrel, that he struck her with a piece of metal, and then choked her. The jury may well decide that, in such a state of blind fury, he was not capable of premeditation."

One newspaper hunted out Saul Price, an outstanding

authority on criminal law and formerly for ten years a member of the Homicide Bureau of the district attorney's office. Mr. Price pointed to the fact that Wayne had confessed to hitting Patsy with *both* candlesticks.

"There was sufficient time between the point when he finished striking her with the first one and the point when he picked up the second one for premeditation," he added. "The pause could have been long enough for him to realize the nature of his act and the power of his blows. Premeditation, therefore, might be shown."

From Nicholas Pecora, law partner of former District Attorney Joab H. Banton, came the opinion that the case was a "very interesting one from a legal standpoint" and that, to him, it hung solely on premeditation. "If Lonergan sticks to his story that he struck her solely in the heat of passion," Pecora declared, "I would say there is every likelihood his case will be one of manslaughter. The only way to prove premeditation, except by his own admission, would be on the basis of testimony by witnesses—and, according to the papers, there were no witnesses."

Mario Gabellini's $10,000 bail was cut in half by Judge Goldstein. It was learned definitely that Patsy Lonergan recently had made a will cutting off Wayne without a cent—thus establishing that money was not the motive for the crime. Lonergan knew of this will. Jacob Grumet, who went into Felony Court and charged his prisoner with the "brutal and unprovoked killing of his wife," asked Magistrate Charles E. Ramsgate to hold Lonergan without bail. He got his wish. Later, Grumet told reporters that Lonergan was bisexual, having the mental characteristics of both sexes, or having sexual desires toward both sexes.

Casual observers pointed out the coincidence that the Burton murder was just one, although the most dramatic one, of a rash of slayings that had taken place that last week in October. In Washington, a baker fired six bullets into the head of his mistress, and later told police, "I wanted to stuff her down that sewer so the rats could eat her." The day after the Lonergan slaying, a six-year-old Lubbock, Texas, girl found her parents murdered. The same day, a young seaman was accused of killing his fourteen-year-old sister-in-law with a shotgun at North Dartmouth, Massachusetts; a defense worker knifed his two sons to death and then shot himself in Gary, Indiana; and in Melbourne, Arkansas, a girl said she had killed her father because he had abused her since she was twelve. A day later, a nurse cadet was found brutally murdered in Poughkeepsie, New York.

It was a bloody week.

Gabellini, out on bail, brought newsmen up to date on his part. He said he had a fourteen-year-old son by Helen Kerns, his first wife, from whom he had been divorced in 1935. Then, he added, he had married Drusilla Dunn, only to divorce her the next year. He denied that he and Patsy had planned to marry after she divorced Wayne, and he said that he had known Lonergan for two years, and had no objections from him over the attention that he, Gabellini, had paid to Patsy.

Up in Toronto, Attorney Lionel Davis went to the provincial attorney general and asked him to probe into the manner in which Lonergan was questioned there for fifteen hours by the police and by Assistant District Attorney Loehr, before being charged with any crime, which procedure, he said, was "wholly improper and illegal."

It was reported that Sylvia French, a Manhattan resident, might be called as a witness in the trial. It was at her home that Lonergan left a toy elephant on the Saturday morning just before the murder. Later, reportedly, he had returned for the plaything and had brought it to Patsy's apartment, in what some officials characterized "an unsuccessful attempt to establish an alibi."

Detectives turned over to the police property clerk two items that undoubtedly would be part of the state's exhibits—a black, eight-pound dumbbell, said to be the mate of the one with which Wayne had weighted down his cadet uniform before tossing it into the East River, and a pair of black-handled scissors in a brown, gold-tooled leather case, taken from John Harjes' apartment, and allegedly used by Wayne to cut up the uniform.

The name of Edward V. Broderick crept into the proceedings for the first time, a name that later dominated the turbulent trial news.

The court had appointed three defense lawyers for the young suspect. Mr. Broderick was named chief of counsel, aided by Millard Ellison and Abraham Halprin. Almost immediately, Broderick indicated that he was not going to be just a figurehead, as court-appointed defense lawyers have so often been. A man with an undeniable flair for publicity, Broderick said that he had been asked by Wayne to look into rumors that Billy Lonergan's name was going to be changed by his grandmother. "He will fight it violently if it is true," Broderick said.

There were the inevitable court delays. The case dropped out of the newspapers for a couple of months. The United States Navy had begun a drive toward the Japanese fleet in the area of the Marshall Islands, and the citizenry had more important things on its mind.

It was the first day of February 1944 when Millard Ellison and Abraham Halprin withdrew from the case as co-attorneys for Lonergan, leaving the defense completely in the hands of Broderick.

To make it official, Lonergan reported to the court that he had acquired sufficient funds to engage his own counsel. How he had acquired enough to pay the costs of a trial that promised to be a long and expensive one, he did not say. He merely reported the name of his new lawyer:

Edward V. Broderick.

As a Yonkers, New York, schoolboy, Edward Broderick scribbled inside his fifth-grade arithmetic book, "Edward V. Broderick, Columbia University, 1912; Columbia Law School, 1915." And Edward Broderick was graduated from Columbia University in 1912, and from Columbia Law School in 1915.

Not since the days of William J. Fallon had any counselor been so involved in stormy scrapes.

Big, burly, blue-eyed, with a cigar forever in his mouth and a habit of rolling his r's, Broderick was completely a criminal lawyer. When he took over Lonergan's defense, he told reporters that he had represented thirty-seven first-degree murder defendants, and had achieved thirty-four acquittals and three manslaughter convictions. He said he looked on criminal law as "the combat competition of the courtroom."

A bachelor who lived with his younger brother, Joe, a former state assemblyman, in an apartment near Columbia University, Broderick had offices at 49 Wall Street. He liked music, poetry, and occasional games of handball, and he had a good working knowledge of Europe, having twice visited the Continent, especially the Riviera, while reportedly tracking down testimony for clients.

When Lonergan hired him as counsel, one reporter said to Broderick, "I understand you're doing this for nothing." Broderick laughed. He never did anything for nothing. Some way, somehow, Edward V. Broderick would profit.

He had come his first cropper with the other side of the bench in January 1926, when a judge found him quilty of contempt of court and imposed a fine, the payment of which he avoided later by purging himself. In 1927 he was defending a cop charged with murder, and he was fined $100 twice in one day for his bull-in-a-china-shop behavior. But his client successfully avoided the first-degree charge and was convicted of manslaughter.

He once told a reporter that he never thought he was the only lawyer in town who could stop a man from getting a raw deal, "but if he's a client of mine, I'll make *sure* he doesn't get one."

In 1929 he got into more hot water. Running (unsuccessfully) for the Democratic leadership in the Thirteenth Assembly District, Broderick rose at a political meeting and charged that Andrew Macrery, a magistrate who had died recently, actually had been beaten to death because of political differences. This charge prompted Broderick's opponent, City Tax Appraiser Andrew T. Keating, to seek an indictment against him on libel charges. The grand jury failed to indict.

Later, in 1947, Judge James G. Wallace was to find Broderick guilty of "studied insolence and defiance" while defending Patrolman Mariano Abello—who got twenty to

life—on the charge of strangling Mrs. Katherine Miller.
Wallace fined him one hundred dollars and five days in
jail on two counts of contempt.

The well-known writer Thyra Samter Winslow, who
was covering the Lonergan trial for one of the New York
newspapers, wrote an open letter to Edward Broderick on
March 3, 1944, his birthday:

Dear Mr. B.:

I do wish you'd learn to control your temper. Oh, I
know how you love to rant and shout that you're being
crucified. And that the Bernheimer millions are trying
to disbar you. And that someone—or something—is trying to put an electric chair in the jury box. And screech
invectives to the Assistant District Attorney. But dear
Mr. Broderick, you're a big boy!

And dear Mr. Broderick, would you for me, stop calling Lonergan "the kid" and "this American boy" and
"young Lonergan"? You never mention his name without prefixing "young." Lonergan is 26, going on 27.
Today a man of 26 is not a kid.

Broderick established the tempo for much of his subse-
quent behavior when, the first time he was scheduled to
confer with his cocounselors, Ellison and Halprin, he de-
ferred the meeting for a day "to investigate some mat-
ters."

At the beginning of February 1944, Ellison and Halprin requested permission to withdraw from the case, and
Judge John G. Freschi granted it. The final straw apparently had been a mysterious cable from the Riviera, "hint-
ing at bizarre international developments," according to
one paper. Ellison and Halprin complained to Judge
Freschi that Broderick had received the cable late in January, and refused to show it to them. Later, when reporters asked Broderick about the cable, he would say
only, "It's been sealed by court order and I can't discuss
it."

Wayne Lonergan had put his life in the hands of a
Yonkers Irishman who customarily just put his head down

defiantly and charged. How much skill Lonergan was hiring was open to debate. It was generally agreed that he had bought himself plenty of noise.

The winter wore on and still the Lonergan trial was delayed. Judge Freschi finally and absolutely set February 23 as the opening date. Broderick, fighting for time—although he announced no vital reason for doing so—had asked for March 15, but this motion had been denied. In making his request, Broderick said he wanted a court-appointed commission to take testimony in Canada, relative to the late Mrs. Clara Lonergan's confinement at various times in the Ontario Mental Hospital.

On Thursday, February 3, Judge Freschi made an announcement that caused commotion in several quarters. He reported that Lonergan had written him a letter saying, "I want to stand trial," and adding that Halprin and Ellison, before pulling out of the defense, had told him that Grumet "on several occasions" had offered him a second-degree murder plea, and would recommend a twenty-to-life sentence. Lonergan wrote that Halprin and Ellison had "urged me very strongly" to accept the offer.

"There was no such conversation," Ellison said flatly, when he heard about the Lonergan letter. "It's a falsehood. We never had any such talk." District Attorney Hogan, asked for comment, contented himself with saying that the letter contained many false statements.

Broderick was finally successful in getting the court to appoint a commission to take the Canadian testimony. On February 11 he again appeared in court with another such motion—this time to have a commission appointed to go all the way to the Panama Canal Zone to take testimony.

This spectacular move was prompted by a letter Lonergan reportedly had received, while in prison, from Jack March, whose real name was John L. Maricini, a Pelham, New York, tennis professional who had been inducted into the Navy and was a seaman stationed at Cristobal. March allegedly wrote to Wayne that he knew of neglect of the Lonergans' baby by Patsy Burton Lonergan.

"I'd have it on my conscience if I didn't try to help you when I could," March told Lonergan, according to Broderick.

The lawyer described March as a former "intimate acquaintance and house guest" of Lonergan's and Patsy's, and said that the seaman's letter told in detail of "how Patsy had neglected your child, all-night parties, loads of people, shouting, etc., when the child was trying to sleep." It went on to say that Patsy "would rush off afternoons and never return until the next day—and all this time you would be with the baby alone.

"I also know how much you love the child and how she would shrug her shoulders when you'd ask her to send her guests home," the letter allegedly continued, adding that March could recall statements "Patsy made about the child in the presence of other parties, etc. Also a few all-night parties in Harlem."

The March letter's real significance, it developed, was that it brought Grumet and Broderick together for the first of their really sharp exchanges. After Broderick moved to have the Canal Zone commission appointed, he then reported that March was "now within reach of New York," and that he might now withdraw his motion altogether.

"There are too many shenanigans going on in this case," Grumet objected heatedly in General Sessions during the argument on the motion before Judge Freschi. "These motions are not made in good faith. They are made to defeat the ends of justice.

"The district attorney's office knows all about March. We smoked him out through his draft board. If necessary, we could have had him in court right now. This defendant is so depraved he has been promiscuous with both men and women. Even now he is planning to lay his bloody hands on his wife's fortune. I'd like to find out the relationship between this man March and Lonergan." Judge Freschi pointed to the impounded and sealed letter.

"If you read this letter," he commented, "maybe you will find out."

Broderick, this same day, again charged that Grumet had offered Lonergan a second-degree plea.

Grumet retorted angrily, "It is not true."

Then Judge Freschi, in not too kindly tones, asked Broderick if he could think of any further reason why the trial shouldn't begin on February 23. Broderick said he might need more time to prepare his defense. Grumet figuratively threw up his hands. "He'll never be ready until he's forced to it," he said.

On February 16, the two attorneys appeared in General Sessions again, to allow Broderick to withdraw his motion for the appointment of a Canal Zone commission. Broderick said March now was in New York, and had reported himself ready at any time to go to the district attorney's office to give information.

Then Broderick blandly asked that Grumet and Loehr submit to lie-detector tests. The veracity of both Grumet and Loehr would be under sustained attack during the trial, he said pleasantly.

Grumet stormed to his feet.

"Your honor!" he cried. "What is the meaning of this? This is becoming a farce. This is a case of murder in the first degree. I'll ask for the mentality of the counsel to be examined."

Judge Freschi glowered. "I won't have this court made a hippodrome," he said.

Broderick seemed unperturbed. In a *non sequitur* of classic proportions, he then asked Grumet "whether he will subpoena the files of the FBI on Elser."

"Why, I thought you were on your own!" Grumet exclaimed indignantly. "Now you're asking for help!"

Broderick turned to Judge Freschi. "I also would like to ask the court to have the District Attorney supply the names of the stool pigeons in the Tombs who talked to Lonergan," he said.

"I'm not making this court a public stage for these requests of counsel," Judge Freschi said tartly. "You can write a letter to the District Attorney, or go to see him."

Broderick then asked if he could ascertain from Grumet the whereabouts of Tim Krusi, the British army-officer friend of Mrs. Lonergan. Grumet objected, and Broderick said disarmingly, "I just don't know whether he is in India or in Africa."

"And you don't know where *you* are!" Grumet shot back.

The Judge banged his gavel.

The day ended with Broderick allowed to withdraw his motion for appointment of a commission.

Two days later Broderick filed another motion. As a result, for the first time the question was raised of whether another person or persons, aside from Wayne Lonergan, had been in that Beekman Hill apartment on the night Patsy Burton Lonergan was beaten to death.

Broderick moved that the judge order the Board of Health and the Medical Examiner to turn over to him (Broderick) a copy of the report of the autopsy performed by Dr. Milton Helpern. "I believe I am entitled to a copy of the autopsy report at the earliest possible moment," he stated, "to learn whether Patricia Lonergan died as a result of criminal means applied by Wayne Lonergan, or another or others, or as a result of natural causes." He stated that he had asked both the Board of Health and the Medical Examiner for such a report, and had been referred to Grumet, who had refused the request. Reporters buttonholed him later. What did this mean? Would Mr. Broderick elaborate?

"I cannot and I will not," the lawyer said curtly.

At the same time, Broderick asked the court to order Lonergan's draft board to release a copy of the psychiatrist's report that had resulted in the suspect's being classified 4-F by the Army. He said that the board, which met in the Hotel Delmonico on Park Avenue, had refused the report to him.

Reporters asked Grumet if he had information that placed someone else in the Lonergan apartment at the time of the murder. No, Grumet said patiently.

But the rumor caught fire despite this denial. Around New York spread the report that there *had* been another person in the apartment during the murder—an unidentified young lawyer friend of Lonergan's. The *World-Telegram* put enough credence in the story to spread it all over page one, topped by the headline CHUM AT KILL-ING BY LONERGAN HINTED, DENIED.

It was a rumor that introduced an angle of the case that was discussed in the town's more elegant men's bars for some weeks. The young lawyer friend reportedly had told intimates that Mrs. Lonergan had attacked Lonergan first, and that she had had her young husband in extreme agony when, in desperation, he had reached for her throat and strangled her. There was little doubt as to the manner of Mrs. Lonergan's attack on Wayne, in this startling version. The story was that she had assaulted him in man's most vulnerable spot. Just how the young lawyer friend happened to be on hand during such an unusual attack was never explained.

Broderick, while aware that rumor held no weight in a courtroom, made capital of this one, and refused to deny the existence of an important new witness. He added that he understood that the District Attorney was investigating "at least along collateral lines."

Grumet could only maintain to reporters that the crime had been committed without witnesses, and disparage the rumor as emphatically as possible.

The *World-Telegram*, dignifying it as "today's report," said that, according to the new story, the young lawyer friend had left the house while Mrs. Lonergan was being strangled and was gone by the time she actually died. "He either came to the Beekman Hill apartment with Lonergan or was there when Lonergan came," the newspaper stated. "In any event, the report is, he was present when the couple quarreled and Mrs. Lonergan scratched and bit her husband." It added that the lawyer had been quoted as saying that Patsy "many times previously" had threatened to attack her husband in the manner described.

The trial date drew nearer, and Broderick continued to try to delay it. On Monday, February 21, he tried a new tack. He said that it was Grumet that wasn't ready.

Broderick appealed again formally for a delay that Monday, and Judge Freschi refused him. Later, Broderick again brought up the third-person-present angle before Judge Freschi. "My information, your honor, is that there was a wealthy, well-known lawyer present," he declared. He also said that he would "like to find out from the *World-Telegram* where they got the information about the third person, that coincides with information I have."

"That's pure, unadulterated nonsense," Grumet said.

Broderick then was denied his other two motions—to get the autopsy report on Patricia Lonergan and to get the draft board's psychiatric record on Wayne Lonergan.

But he was not yet through with his attempts to delay the trial. Wednesday, February 23, rolled around. General Sessions was crammed with two hundred prospective jurors. The long awaited trial seemed about to start.

One important item was missing: Edward Broderick.

It was an angry Judge Freschi that stalked into the courtroom and began the brief proceedings of the day, shortly after ten-thirty A.M. The talesmen had begun arriving more than an hour and a half before, and by ten o'clock had filled virtually every seat in the room. Until then, there had been no requests for spectators' seats, but suddenly a mass of men and women invaded the building, some of them, in haste and confusion, piling into the elevators and riding up to the courtroom on the thirteenth floor of the Criminal Courts Building.

Wayne Lonergan, still in the blue, pencil-striped suit he had worn at his arrest, was brought into an anteroom, kept there for half an hour with three guards, and then returned to prison. Four months of jail *and* the fact that Broderick neglected to visit him the day before the trial was to begin evidently had not left him in the best of shape. His eyes were bloodshot, he picked at his fingers, and he bit his nails.

Shortly after Judge Freschi appeared, Attorney William Merritt, representing Broderick, arose and announced that Broderick was in Canada, and had asked for an adjournment of the case "for all purposes." The judge interrupted. He was well aware that Broderick had gone to Canada, it appeared.

"Mr. Broderick," he said angrily, "has asked for an adjournment for the defendant. He was in court Monday and that adjournment was denied. Mr. Broderick knew that this trial was set for today.

"He left New York City and went to Toronto. He sent me a telegram yesterday saying, 'I'm in Toronto working on information involving the Lonergan case. Unable to be in court February 23. I respectfully ask for an adjournment until February 28.'

"Mr. Broderick said he has not seen the mental-commission report. In addition he makes a request for the re-argument of the autopsy motion.

"I repeat that the mental-commission report was here Monday morning. I had it in my hand and showed it to Mr. Broderick. It was available to him, and as for the second request, I shall not grant any re-argument of that motion."

Judge Freschi's voice rang through the stilled courtroom.

"I have never seen or heard the equal of this," he said. "He has a brother who is a lawyer. According to his own statement, he has two other attorneys in his office. If there was any business in Toronto that required his attention, he could have sent somebody from his office." He glared. "I repeat," he said, "his failure to do so amounts to contempt of court! I intend to deal with that at the close of the trial."

Grumet was almost as angry. He jumped to his feet.

"I ask, Your Honor," he cried, "that Mr. Broderick not be given until the twenty-eighth. I ask simply that the case be put over until tomorrow morning, that the case be marked ready for trial tomorrow, February twenty-fourth." Judge Freschi nodded, scowling.

"The case will be set for tomorrow," he said.

"Instruct his attorneys to wire him to be in court tomorrow morning," Grumet put in.

The Judge pointed out that Broderick had a representative in court. "Let his representative act accordingly," he added.

Later the Judge talked with reporters. He said that he

had received the telegram "at precisely ten-twenty-five
A.M." that day. It obviously was a night letter sent from
Toronto the day before. He refused to release the full text
of the wire. "There are some things in it which constitute
a self-serving declaration," he commented. A reporter
asked the Judge what would happen if Broderick failed
to appear the next day.

"I don't know," the Judge said, angered. "If I were
God, I could tell you. He may come into court and make
a suitable apology. He owes an apology not only to the
court and its officials, but to every juror on the panel. If
he makes that apology, it will be taken into consideration.

"I repeat that his conduct today was the height of improper conduct for a lawyer."

Judge Freschi indicated, however, that if Broderick
failed to appear once more, he probably would have to
permit a further delay.

And, as it developed, Edward Broderick *did* fail to appear once more. Tuesday, February 24, arrived, but he
did not.

There was another telegram, though. This one, also
from Toronto, contained the news that Broderick had received "sketchy reports of today's court proceedings and
that I am not contemptuous of the court.

"I have the highest regard for the jury panel," the
wire read. "I am in dire need of more time to complete
my investigation but the weather and war conditions made
it difficult. When I have finished the investigation in
Toronto, I must spend some time on the international
border." It went on to state that he would be in New
York as early as possible, and in court certainly by the
next Monday morning, February 28, ready for trial.

It was learned that Broderick had been conferring in
Toronto with two Canadian attorneys, retained as ad-
visory counsel by Lonergan's relatives, and reportedly had
interviewed friends and relatives of his client. It also was
reported that he had gone to Buffalo to obtain access to
the records of the Department of Immigration's special
board of inquiry, which had considered Lonergan's entry

into the United States in October—but that he had met
with no success.

The Wednesday proceedings were virtually a repeat
performance. Merritt arose and asked for an adjournment until Monday.

Judge Freschi, evidently overwhelmed by Broderick's
conduct, and with Grumet's irritated consent, put the case
over to Monday.

"I only hope at this time," he added, "that this is not
a challenge of the court or a disregard of the obligations
of a retained private counsel toward his client and the
court."

He referred again to Broderick's conduct as "something
to receive attention at the proper time." Turning to the
170-odd talesmen still on hand, the Judge said he hoped
they would "carry away no false impression that might
prejudice the administration of justice or the rights of the
defendant, who, after all, is entitled to a fair and impartial
trial of the issues, which in this case involve a very serious charge."

It was a judicious statement—but it did not placate the
talesmen. Many of them showed obvious unhappiness. In
addition, it was pointed out that the defense counsel's
absence was costing the taxpayers between $1,200 and
$1,500 a day.

The week end loomed. New York fretted. Broderick's
didoes were absorbing, but the business at hand was the
trial of Wayne Lonergan, and it had been some time
since Manhattan had played host to a first-class murder
trial.

The only important event of the week end was the
recalling of Jean Jaburg from Palm Beach for routine
questioning by Grumet. Evidently there had been talk that
the brown-eyed blonde, Lonergan's companion before and
after the slaying, would be called on to testify that the
defendant had not been rational when she had seen him.
"How could Mrs. Jaburg testify to Lonergan's rationality," Grumet asked, "if he had been drinking heavily when
he was with her, after his wife's death? A man like Loner-

gan could have had six or seven drinks over a period of time, and they might not affect his rationality." Jean, meanwhile, said she had come back only to aid justice.

"This case has ruined my theatrical career," she said. "Previously, I had been talking with several producers about parts. With the publicity I received in this case, everything stopped. I have a family to consider, including an eight-year-old son, and every time my name is brought into this, they suffer."

Nobody commented that Lonergan, too, had a son, or speculated over this child's future.

The week end ended, and Broderick returned from Canada. On Monday, February 28, Wayne Lonergan was brought to trial.

Chapter Five

WAYNE LONERGAN was his old impassive self on the morning of the next-to-last day in a leap-year February when his trial began. His hair had grown out in the four months since his arrest. He wore the pin-striped suit, with a white shirt and a blue polka-dot tie, and he paid close attention to everything that went on.

"I'm ready," Broderick told the newsmen in the corridor before entering court, "but that's all I've got to say."

The trial began at ten-thirty-five A.M. Almost immediately Broderick moved to have Judge Freschi disqualify himself, and to have the blue-ribbon jurors dismissed in favor of a new panel. He did so, he added dramatically, with "the life blood of Wayne Lonergan weighing on my shoulders. . . . As a result of the psychological conditions," he said, "there is a great danger that prejudice has taken root in your subconscious."

Broderick was plaintive, irritated, nervous, and indignant by turns, and denied flatly that he was guilty of contempt. "I had unfinished business in Canada," he explained righteously, "and it was wrong for Mr. Grumet to be supercilious. He showed bad faith from the start." He ended his first outburst by stating that Grumet, at previous hearings, "had asked the court to send me to jail."

Having heard the motion, Judge Freschi asked Grumet for comment. The Assistant District Attorney said that he didn't care to answer the personal accusations, but denied he had asked that Broderick be jailed. The defense counsel was on his feet, shouting. "Your Honor—did or did it not happen?" he demanded loudly.

"I believe I can truthfully say," the Judge said, "that Mr. Grumet did not ask me to put Mr. Broderick in jail." He denied both motions, for disqualification of himself and for dismissal of the panel.

43

Broderick was quickly on his feet with another motion. This time he wanted the contempt proceedings determined before the trial began.

The motion was denied.

But Broderick made still a fourth motion—to have the trial adjourned until March 15. Here he referred to a newspaper report that Lonergan had been discharged dishonorably from the RCAF. "I have a letter dated February nineteenth from the air attaché of the Canadian Embassy to the effect that the Canadian Air Corps will stand behind Lonergan," he said. Broderick added that he needed more time to get character witnesses from Canada, and, almost as an aside, reported that he had information "that a maternal uncle of the defendant is confined in a Midwest insane hospital."

Grumet rose to protest all this. Broderick wheeled and pointed at him. "We were getting along all right until he got hysterical again."

Grumet sighed. "Let's eliminate the nonsense," he said.

But this was only one of many such eruptions.

Broderick's opening-day remarks were all-encompassing. He said he would charge that Lonergan had been tricked into coming here from Canada right after the murder. "The cops told him he was returning to attend his wife's funeral," Broderick shouted. "I say this is deceit and fraud." A little later he said that "they tried to sell Lonergan a plea but they couldn't." And, "They tried to sell me down the river," he said plaintively.

"Mr. Broderick," the Judge interrupted, "don't let the District Attorney get you nervous."

"He's not getting me nervous!" the defense lawyer snapped.

"I told you not to get nervous," Freschi said.

"Who's excited?"

"You're shouting at me," Judge Freschi cautioned.

Finally the Judge directed that the trial begin after a five-minute recess.

Contradicting his earlier statement, Broderick announced to the reporters, "I am not ready and I am being forced to trial, and the defendant cannot get a fair and impartial trial." He then repaired to the corridor and lighted a cigar. Reporters crowded around him in the hope of a further statement. Broderick gave them the startling news that Lonergan had adopted his cigar-smoking habit.

At last, the first talesman's name was drawn from the drum. Immediately before this, however, spectators noted the day's first sign of emotion in Lonergan. Grumet turned and faced the 123 prospective jurors (73 already had been excused). "Ladies and gentlemen," he said, "we are about to try Wayne Thomas Lonergan for murder in the first degree. My name is Grumet and I shall represent the people."

That was all. Sitting at the defense table, Wayne Thomas Lonergan blinked his eyes rapidly, as if for the first time he realized he was on trial for his life. When the first talesman—Solof Schiller, a Park Avenue silk merchant—stepped up, however, Wayne was as impassive as ever.

Only five talesmen were examined that first day, and all of them were excused. Ears pricked when Broderick asked one of them if he would be prejudiced if Lonergan didn't take the stand in his own behalf. It was the first hint that anything of the sort might happen. That night, however, the defense counsel said stoutly that "it wasn't my intention today in court" to create the impression that Lonergan wouldn't take the stand. "I won't say one way or the other," he added thoughtfully.

Newsmen harried him about what his tactics *would* be. He contented himself with saying only that he was ready "for any contingency."

At this point, there was a one-day postponement in the trial. Nobody knew exactly why. Broderick asked for it, and Grumet agreed. Later, Grumet said the postponement had "nothing to do with the case."

But the day—it was a Tuesday—did not go by without incident. In court on Monday, Broderick had referred to a letter allegedly written by Wayne Lonergan on January 25 to Surrogate James A. Foley, offering to give up any claims to his wife's fortune if custody of Billy Lonergan was awarded to the family of the defendant in Canada. The letter said:

> I have read in the newspapers that in my trial for murder in the first degree I am staking my life against two million dollars of the Bernheimer-Burton fortune. My knowledge of that fortune is that it has been unlucky for everyone including myself ever connected with it.
>
> My folks in Canada are in a position to take care of my baby. If Your Honor will agree to have my young son turned over to the exclusive custody of my relations in Canada, I am willing to waive my share and my baby's share of that fortune.

On Tuesday, Grumet unloaded his heavy artillery at the letter. It was not, he announced, mailed until one-thirty P.M. of February 28. This was, roughly, an hour before Broderick referred to it in court, when he asked a prospective juror whether he ever had heard of it, and showed the talesman a copy of it in Broderick's handwriting. That made Broderick's question "not in good faith," Grumet said.

The letter, incidentally, was delivered to Surrogate Foley that Tuesday morning and promptly turned over to the district attorney's office.

"Having been postmarked one-thirty P.M. yesterday," Grumet declared acidly, "it would have been impossible for any of the talesmen to have read about the letter in the papers, or to have heard about it.

"The reason Mr. Broderick wanted the letter impounded was because I had said in court about a week ago that Lonergan was scheming to get his bloody hands on his wife's money."

At the same time, Grumet said that Dr. Perry M. Lichtenstein, a psychiatrist attached to the district attorney's office, had returned from a visit to Canada with evidence that he, Grumet, felt was sufficient to combat any possible defense of hereditary insanity. Broderick's only reference to such a defense during the first day of proceedings had been an oblique one; he had said simply that "the exotic, erotic, and neurotic" might figure in the trial.

On Wednesday, the storm clouds not only gathered; they mushroomed around the ceiling of Special Sessions.

A new hundred-man panel had been recruited overnight to augment the original blue-ribbon group of talesmen, whose ranks had been depleted by excuses. On Wednesday morning the court was so crowded that prospective jurors spilled out into the hall, and Judge Freschi, after calling the roll of the new talesmen, excused them until two days later. Newspapers, meanwhile, had pointed out that morning that the Lonergan letter to Surrogate Foley actually meant little. Under the law, he could not possibly renounce Billy's rights to an inheritance. Furthermore, if he were convicted of murder in the first degree, Lonergan automatically would lose any possible right to a share that he might have.

Broderick suffered his first important setback of the day shortly after the resumption of activity at ten-thirty A.M. Judge Freschi said he wouldn't let defense counsel show prospective jurors the letter to Surrogate Foley.

"I didn't allow the reading of that letter in open court," the Judge said, obviously irritated, "and I didn't mean to have it in the public press. Someone gave it to the press. It couldn't come out of thin air."

Broderick arose. "I consider your remarks highly prejudicial to the defendant," he said. "I protested I didn't want to have the jurors read the letter—"

"*You* protested!" the Judge exclaimed. "Show me a word or a syllable in the record that indicates you protested against any juror seeing the contents of that letter."

Grumet then said he had "serious doubts" as to the authorship of the letter. "In the letter, the defendant—if he wrote the letter—refers to the Bernheimer-Burton fortune," he said. "Isn't it significant that Mr. Broderick constantly uses the same phrase, and doesn't it give us an inkling as to the authorship of the document?"

Up jumped Broderick. Talk bubbled on all sides. It was a while before the hubbub died away.

The sixth prospective juror finally took the stand. Broderick questioned him, then interrupted himself to move that the district attorney furnish him with the names of all the stool pigeons who, he said, had talked with Lonergan in the Tombs. Grumet protested that he was under no obligation to tell defense counsel his witnesses' names. The Judge denied the motion. Broderick, waving his hands, continued what was an obvious attempt to discredit the prosecution witnesses.

Again Judge Freschi's patience deserted him.

"I must warn you," he said to Broderick, "and I can't do anything more at this particular time, not to continue that. Yesterday you made remarks of that nature, and they are all out of order and improper, and counsel should not do this. This is a serious trial. We are here to determine whether Wayne Lonergan murdered his wife."

Grumet leaped angrily to his feet. "I would say," he cried, "that the administration of justice is on trial!"

Arguments continued, on and on. At one point Judge Freschi wearily addressed Grumet. "Can't we eliminate all this? Otherwise, the jurors could go home and I could go to my chambers, and leave you two lawyers to fight it out."

"You don't know Grumet like I do," Broderick said cryptically.

Thursday, March 2, 1944, dawned clear and cold over the city of New York. It was a bright, windy late-winter day. Rain or snow, according to the weather bureau, hung in the offing.

In Special Sessions, the routine began as usual, shortly after ten-thirty A.M. Two prospective jurors were examined. They were excused. Spectators settled grimly in their seats to wait out the tedium.

Then Judge Freschi called Grumet and Broderick up to his bench and held a conference. What they said was lost to most of those present, but those closest to the three men said that Mr. Broderick's comments were interesting. "How long have you been around New York?" he said, at one point, to Grumet. Later: "What about your press agent?" Still later: "You're sticking out your chin. Do you think this is a cream-puff game?" Grumet reddened but kept his temper. The Judge leaned forward and gave him some advice. Grumet then asked formally that Freschi reconsider the motion made Monday by Broderick to discharge the panel.

"May we have the District Attorney's word on the record?" snapped Broderick. "I don't want to be double-crossed." Grumet said tartly that he was asking for reconsideration of the motion because of a story that had appeared in a morning newspaper (the *Daily Mirror*) that had reported that the defense was in possession of "bizarre" pictures of Patsy Burton Lonergan.

"If Mr. Grumet had an ounce of manhood," Broderick said, "he would make a motion himself to dismiss the panel."

Judge Freschi told Broderick that the assistant district attorney "can't do that; you know that."

"Oh, yes, he can, too," Broderick retorted, "if I consent."

Freschi asked Grumet if he would make such a motion. He said he would. Broderick interrupted this to say he was being "short-circuited." Then he fired a broadside.

"I received information last night," he exclaimed dramatically, "that the District Attorney, Frank S. Hogan, was dissatisfied with the way Grumet was handling this case and that he wanted to take him off the case!"

"That's a deliberate lie!" Grumet roared back. "Mr. Hogan feels the same way as I do about the conduct of the defense counsel."

Broderick paid him no heed. "Mr. Grumet," he said, "tried to sell this innocent defendant down the river on a plea, offered in chambers. I say that Mr. Grumet is responding to the pressure of the Bernheimer-Burton millions. He knows he has lost his case.

"About this article in the *Mirror* this morning," he said, "so help me God and may Christ paralyze my tongue— and this is my birthday and that's a terrible oath to take on this day—I had nothing to do with that story!"

They could hear Broderick in the corridors of the building now.

"They couldn't crucify this innocent young man, Lonergan, and they can't crucify me!" he shouted. "If you're a part of it, we might just as well close up the court." As he spoke, he looked directly at Judge Freschi. Then he pounded on the prosecution table.

"The *New York Times* tried to electrocute this boy and let Mr. Sulzberger pull the switch!" he cried.

This, apparently, was a reference to a story in the Monday *Times,* to the effect that Lonergan had been discharged dishonorably from the Royal Canadian Air Force. The story, the *Times* reported later, was based on a statement from an RCAF officer who, it developed, was not authorized to speak for the unit.

Broderick pulled out all the stops.

"The Bernheimer-Burton seven-million-dollar estate and the *New York Times* have ganged up on me! This is only the foundation for proceedings to disbar me."

Finally the diatribe was over. The court buzzed with excited conversation. Judge Freschi rapped for order, and then he looked over at Broderick.

"Now, Mr. Broderick," he said smoothly, "after that long speech in which you showed considerable emotion, I'd like to know if you do consent to the discharge of this panel."

The defense counsel, it developed, had only been getting his second wind. He bounded up.

"If Mr. Grumet gives me the murder list that he holds in his office," he said loudly, "I'll take the first twelve names on this panel, if they are not on the guaranteed murder list. The District Attorney has all kinds of money; this kid hasn't a dime."

"This kid" sat impassively, watching his lawyer in operation.

Broderick continued. "You talk about wasting six hundred dollars a day of the taxpayers' money—now don't talk about the six hundred dollars a day!" he shouted. "It wasn't my fault last Thursday. There is a limit to physical endurance. I say, if they want to crucify this boy, don't let them do it! I want an American trial! I'll not consent!"

Judge Freschi sighed and spoke gently to Broderick about his "unwarranted excitement and ungentlemanly conduct."

"You should calm yourself," he said. "We have a duty to perform." Then he announced that he would study the legality of reconsidering Mr. Broderick's motion to discharge the panel. If he could, he added, he would declare a mistrial.

"My license to practice law," Broderick roared, when the Judge had finished, "isn't worth anything under these conditions—and if you want it, I'll give it to you right now!"

After a moment, he apologized to Judge Freschi. "It wasn't meant to be ungentlemanly conduct," he said contritely. Then, at last, the courtroom was cleared and the trial adjourned. Broderick went over to his client and grasped his hand. The other members of the defense counsel seemed pleased at the day's proceedings. Out in the corridor, Grumet talked to newsmen.

"I will not go into the gutter with Mr. Broderick," he said. He added that it wasn't only the *Mirror* story that prompted him to ask that the panel be discharged. It was, he said, a "cumulative" series of events.

"I have felt right along," Grumet declared, "that this case should be disposed of as expeditiously as possible. I still feel that way.

"In the light of the widespread publicity this case is receiving and the fact that it is being watched as it is by so many people, the conduct of counsel for the defense from the very outset has been an affront to the court and a blow against the administration of justice."

The legality of declaring a mistrial immediately touched off a storm of controversy among attorneys and judges throughout the Criminal Courts Building. Some said no mistrial could be declared until a juror or a witness was sworn. Others said the prosecution could not legally force a mistrial on the defense without consent.

Grumet, asked what he would do if his motion were

granted, said that he would move as soon as possible to appoint a special panel. Did that mean a new judge? "I don't think so," he replied.

At the Bar Association, when the day's fury had abated, a spokesman said that no disbarment proceedings had been instituted against Broderick. Such proceedings, he added, could be undertaken only after the trial. Newsmen tried without success to read a prediction in the spokesman's eyes or voice.

Thus far in the Lonergan trial, the mien of Judge Freschi had been reasonably calm.

On the morning of Friday, March 3, he was one hour and seven minutes late ascending the bench. When he finally did so, it was obvious immediately that his mild manner was gone.

There was a brief memorandum on the desk in front of him. He glanced at it. There was no need for the court attendant to rap for order. The talesmen—from both the original and the special panels—had been fidgeting in packed discomfort. Now the buzz of whispering and talking ended abruptly.

"Several days ago," the Judge announced, "counsel for the defense made a motion for dismissal of the panel on the grounds that the rights of the defendant had been prejudiced.

"At that time, I denied the motion. Yesterday the District Attorney announced he had no objection, and made the application for me to reconsider. He stated he would consent to the granting of the motion.

"In spite of his vehement denunciation several days ago, and vociferous arguments that a fair trial could not be had, counsel for the defense did a right-about-face and asserted that he wouldn't accept the District Attorney's consent on the motion."

The Judge glared.

"Since the defendant's counsel made the motion to dismiss the panel," he went on, "and since the District Attorney has consented thereto, I grant that motion."

The Lonergan trial had come to a stop.

The Judge continued. Although Broderick's motion originally had been based on the defense counsel's belief that a fair trial was impossible, Freschi made it clear that this was not the reason for his action.

His decision, he said, "is made apart and separate" from Broderick's reason. He then turned to Broderick, who sat at the defense table, and who, all through the Judge's statement, had been talking with his brother Joe.

"His [Broderick's] attitude has persuaded me that he has attempted to make of this trial a farce and mockery," the Judge said loudly and sharply, "all for purposes which I cannot fathom.

"He prefers to proceed to delay and interfere with the administration of justice.

"His conduct has been such that it seems to me that it has been adequate in my mind to raise the question whether his statements, demeanor, and entire attitude have not so beclouded the issues in this case that there is a danger that the jurors ultimately selected from this panel might find it difficult to evaluate the evidence and the relevant facts, and therefore the defendant might be prejudiced."

The Judge deplored the expense to which the state had been put in calling talesmen. "However," he added, "there is a human life involved and those other things must take second place in our consideration."

There was, he said, no question of double jeopardy, since the jury had not been sworn. He then said he discharged "each of the ladies and gentlemen whose names appear on this panel"—and then Broderick made his move.

"May I be heard?" he began—and *bang!* Down came the gavel.

"No!" Judge Freschi exclaimed.

Broderick was undaunted. "You said—"

"No, no, no!" Judge Freschi shouted, slapping the bench before him with his open hands. Broderick promptly asked if he could take exception to "your refusal to hear me at this time on your wording of the decision here."

"Yes, that is the way to do it," the Judge began—but Broderick cut in again.

"—because it is a continuation of Mr. Grumet's attempts to harrass me, which are prejudicial to my client." The Judge told him to sit down.

"I propose," the Judge said, with steel in his voice, "to have counsel show cause before me why he should not be held in contempt." He said he would fix next Friday, one week from then, as a hearing date for contempt proceedings. If Broderick did not answer, he said, he would direct that specifications be drawn up.

"May I have an objection?" Broderick exclaimed heatedly. "As it will prejudice my client—"

"Wait a minute, Mr. Broderick," the Judge said. Broderick continued talking, making some mention of "jail."

"I have *not* said anything about putting anybody in jail!" the Judge shouted, again slamming his desk.

"I don't care what happens to me—" Broderick began. Freschi blew his top.

"Hold up, *hold up!*" he yelled. "Now, be *seated!* I'm not going to let you, Mr. Broderick, use this courtroom for a vaudeville stage. You must act like a lawyer is expected to act. Be *seated*, Mr. Broderick!"

Above the muffled roar in General Sessions rose the trumpeting voice of Edward Broderick, the undaunted.

"Are you going to let this defendant *rot* in jail?" he demanded.

"The matter of the trial date is to be fixed by the District Attorney when he puts the case on the calendar," the Judge said. Then he sighed. "And I hope this case will not be brought to trial before me as presiding judge."

At this point, District Attorney Hogan, who had been virtually silent in the weeks up to now, arose. He expressed admiration for the Judge's "great patience," and added:

"I now ask that Your Honor direct that all the records and proceedings in this case, both in court and in chambers, be sent to the Appellate Division of this department for appropriate action."

The Judge granted the motion and adjourned the trial.

The customary postproceeding quizzing began, and reporters surrounded the principals. Broderick appeared highly nervous as he announced that he was doing his very best to get justice for Wayne Lonergan.

"The way has become very hard," he said, "not because of anything I did, but because of things others wanted done."

When asked how he felt about the contempt citation, he shrugged. "I'm slated to get thirty days regardless, aren't I?" he asked.

Another little knot of newsmen surrounded Hogan and Grumet. Hogan said that he wanted to clear up the situation regarding Grumet. "That [Broderick's charge that Hogan was dissatisfied] is just rubbish," he said. "I have always had the highest respect for Mr. Grumet's ability, and I have approved of everything he has done in this case." When the trial was resumed, he added, Jack Grumet still would be the prosecutor.

Finally Broderick pushed his way through the crowd to Hogan's side. "Frank," he said, "I'll be very glad to meet you at the Appellate Division."

"I'm sorry I had to make the remarks I did," Hogan said urbanely, "but circumstances made it necessary."

Broderick smiled. "I think you're wrong," he said. "I'll be up at the Appellate Division. I will lick you."

Feelings appeared soothed, and the furor was dying down. Only a very few in General Sessions paid any attention to the tall, good-looking young man, his face as masklike as ever, who was led out of the courtroom by uniformed guards, to be returned to the Tombs.

A little later Broderick too went to the Tombs, and conferred at length with his client. When he emerged, he handed a note to newsmen, without comment. It was written in pen and ink and it read:

125 White Street
March 3, 1:55 P.M.

All I want is a fair trial. I am sorry my trial has been delayed. I have complete faith and confidence in Mr. Broderick.

WAYNE LONERGAN

Chapter Six

THERE WAS a few days' lull. On Wednesday of the next week, March 8, the principals appeared once more in General Sessions. Edward Broderick was unusually restrained and even-tempered.

Within five minutes, a motion had been made and granted for the drawing of a special panel of talesmen. Broderick made one small attempt to block the motion. He handed Judge John A. Mullen an affidavit opposing the motion, on the ground that a blue-ribbon panel violated Lonergan's constitutional rights. He made a brief speech to the effect that there seemed to be "one brand of justice for Westchester and another for New York City." Mullen eyed him.

"Anything else?" he asked. Broderick, startled, just stood there.

"Motion granted," the Judge said.

In a matter of minutes, the courtroom was cleared, and Grumet told newsmen that the trial would start March 20. Judge Freschi got his wish. The judge at the new trial would be James G. Wallace.

Judge Freschi, however, did sit in General Sessions later that day, long enough to adjourn until April 14 the contempt proceedings against Broderick. He took the opportunity to have read into the record a long statement condemning the widespread publicity the case had received.

"I had been considering barring the public from the trial after the jury would have been selected—except the press representatives," Judge Freschi said. "Morbid curiosity seems to have taken hold of some people.

"What people should have more of are the details of decent living and the simple virtues of life and of wholesome instincts and habits of piety, rather than the worthless and aimless monotony of some of those who have been called in this case the café society."

The "second" trial of Wayne Thomas Lonergan began Monday morning, March 20. Nearly five months had passed since Patsy Lonergan had been found bludgeoned and strangled to death. On this same Monday, two dozen people were drowned when a bus plunged into a New Jersey river, and Russia's First and Second Armies of the Ukraine drove German troops into headlong retreat into Rumania and the Carpathian foothills—but the Lonergan murder case was still the page-one banner story in the papers.

In sharp contrast to the previous circus atmosphere, proceedings went swiftly and calmly. By twelve-thirty P.M., three jurors already had been selected. William J. Byrne, an insurance-company claim examiner, was the first, and he automatically became foreman. During the questioning of panelists, Judge James Garrett Wallace spent most of his time leafing almost idly through a copy of the *Law Journal*. Once in a while he paused to direct the questioning.

Broderick scored what seemed to be the first victory of the new proceedings. He asked the Judge to instruct Grumet to disclose the names of possible witnesses. Judge Freschi had refused a similar request. Judge Wallace said, "That's a good idea. Let's do it." Grumet objected, on the grounds that he did not have a complete list, but the Judge told him to "tell all you can think of and send a man down to get the rest of them." Grumet then listed the following:

Dr. Milton Helpern, assistant medical examiner
William Loughram, unidentified further
Mr. Trawitz, unidentified further
John F. Harjes
Mrs. Jean Murphy Jaburg
Jack March
Emil Petters, the Harjes butler
Mrs. Emil Petters
Elizabeth Black, the governess
Mrs. Lucille Burton Wolfe
Captain Peter Elser
Mario Gabellini

Mr. Vaccaro, unidentified further
Ruth Forster, daughter of a Lexington Avenue florist
Miss Schonberg, unidentified further
Policemen: Captain Daniel Mahoney of the Homicide Squad; Detectives Nicholas Looram and William Prendergast; Acting Deputy Chief Inspector Patrick J. Kenny; and a Lieutenant Brennan.

It appeared highly likely that defense counsel would bring up insanity during the course of the trial. Dr. Thomas S. Cusack, the Brooklyn psychiatrist engaged by the defense, had visited Lonergan twice over the week end. Cusack had figured prominently in the testimony during the Snyder-Gray and Nancy Titterton murder cases.

Tuesday, March 21, saw the same down-to-brass-tacks atmosphere in the courtroom. The selection of jurors continued smoothly. One talesman, ad salesman Don Whiting, was excused because he said he had bet even money that Lonergan would be convicted of murder in the first degree.

Now that the trial seemed actually under way, Lonergan once again overshadowed the courtroom. One newsman wrote:

> They get around too much, these members of what must be called the Younger Generation, ever to lose their aplomb completely. At seven they know which fork to use. At thirteen they know the difference between a daiquiri and a bacardi. At twenty they've lived a harsh lifetime.
>
> So with Wayne Lonergan.
>
> He is outwardly poised as he sits in General Sessions on trial for murdering the woman he married. There is this change—the veneer is gone. That what-the-hell attitude is gone. The pseudo tomorrow-we-die air is gone. Lonergan knows that tomorrow he *may* die. There is a difference, now. . . .
>
> The poise has been ground into him for keeps, but he has no time to be flip. Living was rich and cheap to him once; now suddenly it is sparse and dear. For

all the shame on his head, for all the talk of his sexual
aberrations, he doesn't want to die.

So he doesn't miss a trick.

He sits straight in his leather chair, his long legs
stretched, ankles crossed, under the defense table. His
arms are folded, or perhaps his hands are on the table
before him. The ring on his left little finger glints dully.
His blue suit could use a pressing.

He is handsome; many movie heroes are less attractive. A strong chin, a Grecian nose, dark brown hair,
small ears, a face white as paper. It is the face of a
gladiator. There is no tremble to the jutting lower lip.
No tightening of the jaw muscles. He just sits there.
Only the eyes give him away at all.

You wonder, as you watch him sitting there, where
you have seen that expression before, and then you remember. It was the face of a boy who had just stum-
bled from a car he had smashed against a pole, killing
two young girls. It was calm but serious, with curious
intensity in the eyes.

You remember thinking that day that life suddenly
had caught up with that boy—that the ennui, the bore-
dom, the fake excitement, the imitation of life had
ended. It was the real thing, that gray morning, and
when he stood there and said "Gee," you realized the
veneer of a heedless, insensate generation was gone.

The jury was completed, with two alternates, by the
afternoon of Tuesday.

On Wednesday morning, Assistant District Attorney
Grumet made the prosecution's opening address. Forty-
three newspapermen were in the room, along with eight-
een spectators, one of whom was Mrs. Grumet. Before
the proceedings began, court attendants told reporters
that the Judge wanted a minimum of spectators in the
room, and that there was "every chance" the trial ultimately might be closed to everyone but the press.

Grumet began: "The indictment which was read to
you at the very outset charged that the defendant killed
his wife, Patricia Burton Lonergan, on October twenty-

four, 1943, by beating, choking, and strangling her in her apartment at Three-thirteen East Fifty-first Street in this county. I propose at this time to briefly outline for you what the people will prove in support of this charge."

Slowly, carefully, as if he were lecturing a class, Grumet described the events leading up to and after the murder. Almost immediately he scotched, so far as he was concerned at least, the report that there had been a third person present in the flat. "We have only the statement of this defendant as to what transpired there just before he killed her," he stated. "His wife, the only other person in the room at the time, is dead."

He spared no detail in describing the death scene as he and the police had reconstructed it. He told how, in the state's opinion, Lonergan broke one candle holder over Patsy's head, then got the second holder. Some observers felt he emphasized this point because of the District Attorney's desire to prove premeditation.

"He then returned to the bed," Grumet said, "where he rained more blows on his wife's head and face.

"By this time, the deceased was in a sitting position and was bleeding profusely. He had fractured her skull. In an effort to get away from the defendant, she managed to get out of bed on the side opposite to where the defendant was standing. She tried to defend herself, but to no avail. He was determined to kill her. He went after her, going around the bed and grabbing her by the throat with both of his hands. He strangled her for a considerable length of time, until her body was lifeless."

Grumet then proceeded to block in Lonergan's actions after the slaying. When he came to Lonergan's version of the encounter with the soldier, and of being scratched and robbed by him, Grumet said, distastefully it seemed, "I do not believe that it is necessary to go into the sordid details of the story of degeneracy that he told in connection with it. He later repudiated these stories as entirely false and admitted that he had lied."

He then finished his talk quickly, and Broderick rose to address the jury on behalf of the defense.

"We will show you," Broderick began, "that the defendant, Lonergan, from the very inception of this case has been a victim of double dealing, double crossing, and double talk, double talk such as was illustrated in your own presence by only giving partial names, by—"

Judge Wallace and Grumet jumped on him almost simultaneously. "Mr. Broderick," the Judge said patiently, "this is the time for the opening. The purpose of an opening is to tell the jury what you expect to prove."

Broderick nodded.

"On the premise, gentlemen, that you are aware of what has happened in your presence," he said to the jury, "I intend to make the briefest opening address that I have made in twenty-nine years of practice here—and I am doing that as a protective device, not to protect guilt, but to protect innocence, against this double-dealing, double-crossing double talk."

And that was it. One minute and eight seconds was all that Broderick had needed for his opening.

The first witness was William Loughram, an engineer in the district attorney's office. Broderick conceded his qualifications. Then Loughram identified a large cardboard diagram, perhaps half again as big as an office desktop, as one he had drawn of the Lonergan apartment after the murder. It was marked "People's Exhibit 1" and Loughram, standing before it, traced each detail of the apartment.

Broderick, cross-examining, checked and cleared up a few items. Then:

Q. Did you examine the furniture in bedroom number two [the western front bedroom] and its location?

A. I will tell you what was in there.

Q. If you would, please.

A. There was a single wooden bed, a single bed.

Judge Wallace interrupted. "What is the materiality of all this, Mr. Broderick?" he asked. "Is anything supposed to have happened there with regard to this case in those bedrooms?"

Broderick replied smoothly, "It may become material

later on, Judge, and I will be very brief on it." But he had little more to add to this line of questioning and Loughram was excused.

Chris Trauerts, a patrolman attached to the photograph section of the Bureau of Criminal Identification, was the second witness. He told of taking photographs of the murder room, and of the position of the body on the bed. There were six photographs in all. Broderick took them over to the defense table, and Wayne Lonergan, as pale and expressionless as ever, leaned over to see them.

Third on the stand was Dr. Milton Helpern, an assistant medical examiner. He described himself to Grumet as a man who had performed about 6,500 autopsies in his thirteen years with the medical examiner's office. Then he told, in the unemotional, uncompromising language of the physician, of the bloody scene in the Beekman Hill apartment.

The nude body of the girl on the bed, Dr. Helpern said, was that of a young white woman. The head lay toward the foot of the bed, up against the baseboard. It was lying on its left side, the knees bent slightly, the thighs bent slightly. *Rigor mortis,* he added, was complete, indicating that Patsy Lonergan had been dead for some time. This, he said, could have been anywhere from eight to fifteen or sixteen hours, "or even longer or even shorter than that."

The head, Dr. Halpern went on, was bloody, the hair matted. There were three "obvious" lacerations of the scalp; from these blood had soaked through the blanket and mattress and had left a dried pool on the floor. "The left hand of the deceased," he said, "showed a bruise on the middle finger. There were also marks of injury on the neck. There was a series of abrasions and small linear scratches and some bruising of the skin of the neck."

There was dry blood on the shoulders, Dr. Helpern said. On the floor was a pillow stained with blood, and under the pillow he had found a broken-off fingernail. On the other side of the bed he had found another fragment of fingernail, which subsequently proved to be artificial. It was split down the middle.

At this point, Grumet introduced as people's exhibits the fragments of the shattered candlesticks. Then Dr. Helpern proceeded to the autopsy, which he said he had performed the day after the slaying, in the city mortuary on East 29th Street.

All the injuries, the autopsy disclosed, were on the head and in the area of the neck, Dr. Helpern said. It was a combination of these injuries—each of which he described in technical detail—that had caused death.

Broderick cross-examined, evidently without a set pattern in mind, chiseling away here and there at little facts. He won from Helpern the statement that possibly Patsy Burton had been dead less than the five or six hours he had given as a bottom limit. Then he questioned the doctor in detail about the technical details of an autopsy. Women in the courtroom whitened a little as Helpern spoke of using a carpenter's saw, a hammer, and a chisel to take the top of the head off. When the Judge said he thought there had been about enough of that, Broderick asked about the deep wound in Patsy Burton's skull.

"Could it also have been caused by a whisky bottle in a night club fifteen hours before?" he asked. When Judge Wallace excluded that question, Broderick asked if any bottle, empty or full, could have caused the injury. Helpern said he didn't think so.

Broderick asked Dr. Helpern if any alcohol had been found in the dead woman's brain.

A. The brain was examined, a portion of it was distilled, and a two-plus amount, which is a fair amount of alcohol, was found in the brain, which would indicate that the deceased had been drinking some time before death. Two-plus amount is the amount of alcohol in the brain. They are designated as follows: a trace, meaning a very slight amount, one-plus, and two-plus, which are moderate amounts, and then three-plus and four-plus, which are the amounts one finds in intoxicated persons, and those are the grades that are used, the designations that are used. This woman had a two-plus amount, which would indicate that she was drinking.

The witness was excused finally, and Frieda Casseur, who worked for Patsy Burton's grandparents in Elberon, New Jersey, told briefly of identifying the body. The trial then was adjourned until the next morning.

On Thursday there was a delay at the outset of fifteen minutes. Grumet was late, which evidently didn't set too well with Judge Wallace, who had been eying the black-and-gold clock over the rear door for several minutes. The Judge conferred with the prosecutor briefly at the bench before proceedings began; as he spoke, the Judge's eye traveled frequently to the clock.

The first witness of the day was Patrolman John J. Casey of the East 51st Street station—the first officer to arrive at the murder scene. He detailed how he had gone to the apartment at eight-ten P.M., in response to a radio alarm, had met Captain Elser, and had been taken to the bedroom. As he spoke, Broderick motioned to Lonergan, seated two chairs away from him at the defense table. Wayne leaned across Joe Broderick, the attorney's brother, listened intently, wrote a single word on a sheet of paper, and passed it over to Broderick. He returned to his relaxed posture, blinking constantly, but impassive.

Elizabeth Black next took the stand.

The sixty-year-old nurse for Billy Lonergan, speaking carefully and almost timidly, never looked at the defendant. Seventeen spectators, including eight women—two of them elderly, dignified, white-haired ladies dressed in black—were in the courtroom as Elizabeth Black told of going to work for the Lonergans on January 13, 1943, at their Park Avenue apartment, after having worked for seven years for a family in Long Branch, New Jersey.

Yes, she remembered the day of the murder, she told Grumet. "At half past two I went to Mrs. Lonergan's door and I said, 'Young woman, are you going to sleep all day?'—joking."

Q. You say you went to her door?
A. I went to her door and tried the handle and it was locked.

Q. Yes?

A. So then I went on, and the boy, little Billy, was awake, so I went in, got him dressed, and took him to his grandmother's at about three o'clock.

Q. That was Sunday afternoon?

A. That was Sunday afternoon.

She had returned home at five-twenty, she went on. Then she got Billy his supper, bathed him, and let him "play around for a little while." At six-forty-five she put him to bed.

A. So then I sat reading the paper a little while until he went to sleep. Then I wondered why she hadn't got up, and I went back to the door and I touched the door with my toe.

Q. Did what?

A. Touched the door with my toe.

It was then that she called Mrs. Burton, Patsy's mother. Mrs. Burton, she went on, came over about twenty-five minutes later. While she waited, she testified, Captain Elser called, and as she talked to him on the phone, Mrs. Burton entered. She asked Miss Black who was on the phone. When the nurse told her, Mrs. Burton took the phone. After she had spoken a while, she put the receiver down, but she did not break the connection. She and Miss Black went up to the bedroom, and they both knocked on the door.

A. Mrs. Burton called, "Patsy, what is wrong?"

Q. Yes?

A. Well, then, can I say that Mrs. Burton turned to me and said, "You know Patsy is in the country?"

Q. No.

Captain Elser, she said, "was still hanging on the telephone." Then Mrs. Burton returned and spoke some more to him. Ten or fifteen minutes later, Elser arrived at the apartment. He asked Patsy's mother if she wanted the door broken in and Mrs. Burton said yes, whereupon the Marine captain broke it in partially, then got a hammer and knocked the door from its hinges until it fell all the way in.

Q. Now, after the door was taken off its hinges, what, if anything, did you do?

A. Mrs.—

Q. Or what did the others do?

A. Captain Elser said to Mrs. Burton, "Go into the nursery," and I went into the bedroom with Captain Elser.

Q. Yes?

A. And when I went into the bedroom I saw the bed and Captain Elser said, "There is nobody here." He walked another step or so and then I think he said, "Good God," or "My God," and he rushed back and he said, "Go and keep Mrs. Burton in the nursery." He went downstairs and after that I heard the policemen come.

Grumet showed Miss Black four police photographs of the scene that she had come upon in the bedroom, and asked her if they represented it accurately. The nurse put on her glasses and studied them carefully, still biting her lips.

"Yes," she said, barely audibly.

Broderick took up his cross-examination.

Q. Prior to seeing Mrs. Lonergan's body on the evening of October 24, 1943, when was the last time you saw Mrs. Lonergan?

A. On Saturday, about two o'clock.

Q. That is, two o'clock in the afternoon?

A. In the afternoon, Saturday.

Q. Where did you see her at that time?

A. In her bedroom, getting dressed to go out to lunch.

Q. And what time did she go out to lunch?

A. Around two.

Q. That was the last time you saw her alive?

A. That was the last time.

Patsy Lonergan went out to lunch alone at that time, Miss Black added. Before two that day, she had not seen her mistress, "because I go out in the mornings and come back with the child, and I was just coming up the stairs." She did not know, she said, when Mrs. Lonergan returned home after two P.M. Saturday. On Sunday, October 24, Elizabeth Black said, she arose about seven-thirty A.M. Actually she had awakened earlier, at six, to give Billy his orange juice, as usual. Then she went back to bed. By eight-thirty or eight-forty-five she had finished giving Billy his breakfast and washing and dressing him. Broderick asked whether the bathroom used for bathing Billy was the same one used by Mrs. Lonergan. "Oh, no," Miss Black said, as if horrified at the idea.

She did not notice whether Mrs. Lonergan's door was open or shut at that time, she said.

Q. What time did Marie Tanzosch [the maid] come to work that day?

A. She didn't come on Sunday at all, because it was her day off.

Q. [*By Judge Wallace*] At any time, from the time you went to bed on Saturday night until you woke up at six o'clock Sunday morning, did you hear any noise?

A. No, I did not.

Q. You sleep pretty sound, do you?

A. Yes, I do.

Q. Did you hear any voices that you recognized, either in the apartment or in the public hallway or right in front of the building?

A. No, I did not.

At ten A.M., Miss Black went on, she took Billy downstairs to the basement, bundled him into his carriage, and took him "around the block." She walked over to the East River, then pushed the carriage around "for an hour or so"—it was cold and windy, she recalled—and returned to the house just before noon.

"I saw no one in the basement," she said. "I put the carriage away, took Billy up to his play pen, and I went down and got him his lunch and brought it up. I stayed with him for a while, and then I went down and ate and came up again."

At one-thirty, she said, Mario Gabellini called. Broderick doggedly tried to draw in Gabellini's personal relations with Patsy Lonergan, but Judge Wallace balked him. He asked Miss Black if the decorator ever had given Billy or his mother presents, but the Judge excluded any answers.

Around three o'clock, the governess resumed, she took Billy to visit his grandmother—Mrs. Housman, who lived at the Hotel Elysee—"because I thought Mrs. Lonergan was sleeping and didn't want to be disturbed." She returned about six or six-thirty, then fed Billy and put him to bed.

Redirect examination by Grumet, dealing with technicalities of the apartment, followed, and finally the nurse left the stand.

Lucille Wolfe Burton was the next to testify. Dressed in black, with a black felt hat and veil and a mink coat with cape attached, she was a handsome woman, her upswept brown hair streaked with gray.

She was on the stand for less than ten minutes. She substantiated Miss Black's story, under Grumet's questioning—and then Broderick waived cross-examination. Mrs. Burton's feelings about Wayne Lonergan already had been well publicized.

Pete Elser followed Patsy's mother to the stand. The one-time Harvard football star was an impressive figure. On inactive duty from the Marine Corps, he was powerfully built, with spectacles and a mustache, and wore a double-breasted blue suit and a blue shirt.

Elser told of coming to the Lonergan's apartment, of being met by a nervous and excited Mrs. Burton, and of first trying a key to the bedroom door and discovering that it stuck. "I knew the door was locked on the inside," he added. When he finally removed the door from the hinges and walked in, he said, two lights were on and "at first I saw nothing unusual." Then he saw the body on the bed. It was the first time, he told Judge Wallace in answer to a question, that he ever had been in Patricia Burton Lonergan's apartment.

Q. Now, by the way, when was the last time that you saw Mrs. Lonergan alive?

A. On Thursday night, October 21st.

Q. And where was that?

A. At El Morocco, sir.

Q. Was that a chance meeting, or by appointment?

A. A chance meeting, sir.

Q. And when had you seen her prior to that?

A. Why, I was in college two and a half years before that, in March 1941.

Q. In other words, you saw her prior to your meeting her at El Morocco by chance on Thursday night, two and one-half years prior to that, is that right?

A. No, sir. I saw her in March 1941; the last time I saw her was at Franconia Notch, New Hampshire, skiing.

Q. Was she married at the time?

A. No, sir.

Cross-examining, Broderick asked Elser if he had been discharged from the Marine Corps "for medical reasons or anything like that?" but Judge Wallace excluded the question. Then defense counsel pursued the item of the "chance meeting" at El Morocco, the celebrated supper club on East 54th Street.

Patsy, Captain Elser said, was with some other people at the club, one of whom—a girl named Frederica Patterson—he had met before. "I bumped into her [Mrs. Lonergan] on the dance floor and she asked me to dance with her, which I did, and then I took her back to her table," Elser declared. That was the extent of his "interview with her at that time," the Marine officer replied. He did not make an appointment to meet her later, but said she had told him her phone was in the book under the name of Fentress, the man from whom the Lonergan apartment had been rented.

Q. Mr. Elser, did Mrs. Lonergan give the name of the

man with whom she was dancing when you met her on the floor of El Morocco?

Q. (*by Judge Wallace*) Did you know him?

A. I was introduced to him, sir; I didn't remember the name at the time.

Q. Do you remember his name now?

A. Yes.

Q. (*by Grumet*) I object to that.

Q. (*by Judge Wallace*) What difference does it make? Excluded.

Q. (*By Broderick*) I can't disclose my whole case, Judge.

Q. (*by Judge Wallace*) Well, if it is so important, what *was* his name? Do you know?

A. Gabellini.

Q. That is all.

So much for the morning session. In the afternoon, Judge Wallace again spoke sharply to Grumet for arriving late in the courtroom. "I have to take care of the witnesses," Grumet complained.

"You take care of them and get here before I get here," Wallace said testily.

Hedley Ashley, a detective assigned to the photographic bureau of the Toronto Police Department, was the first afternoon witness. Photographs that he had taken of Lonergan at Toronto's criminal identification bureau were introduced as evidence, after Broderick had protested that "no proper foundation had been laid." The Judge questioned Ashley, who, it developed, had taken one hundred thousand photographs in more than thirty years' work with the Toronto police. That seemed foundation enough. The pictures were admitted.

At the time he took the pictures, Detective Ashley said, he had noticed "a slight scratching underneath the chin" on Lonergan's face. Broderick, cross-examining, asked if Lonergan had been brought to Ashley from a cell in Toronto's police headquarters—evidently trying to suggest that the scratches might have been caused after Lonergan had returned to Canada from New York—but Judge

Wallace brushed that aside with "It doesn't make a particle of difference as far as I can see."

Next on the stand was John Frederick Harjes, who had lent his apartment to Lonergan on the fateful week end.

Harjes, as writer Helen Worden of the *World-Telegram* pointed out, "looked and acted his background, that of a man shielded from the world by great wealth." Shirt, tie, suit, and socks were a symphony of brown. He spoke with a British accent, with Oxonian overtones. Harjes' father, the late Colonel Henry Harjes, head of the J. P. Morgan banking firm in Paris, had been French. His mother, Mrs. Seton Porter, was a Berwind of Philadelphia. Her handsome son had been tutored by Englishmen.

It was during Harjes' testimony that a stranger appeared and tried to crash the courtroom. Singling out one court attendant, the stranger announced brusquely that he was a government secret agent ordered to get the testimony of a certain witness, presumably Harjes. Court attendants were unmoved by this information. The stranger then said that he was working for a private detective agency, and, to carry out this line of attack, he flashed a badge, quickly enough to forestall close examination.

"Well, I'll tell that information to the Judge," an attendant volunteered dubiously—and the stranger hurried off, to be seen no more.

Harjes began by stating he had known Lonergan "on and off" for four years. Then he said that Wayne had come to his apartment at three A.M. on Saturday, October 23, after having telephoned from Canada and asked if he could use the apartment. Later that morning he saw Wayne at breakfast, and still later in the day, he testified, he introduced him to Jean Murphy Jaburg, when Lonergan "asked me if I knew of a girl that would like to go out with him."

At six-fifteen P.M., Harjes said, he left his apartment "to go and stay with some friends." He returned the next evening, between ten and ten-fifteen P.M. It was then, he said under Grumet's questioning, that he found on the blotter of his desk the letter from Lonergan, which read:

"John: Thank you so much for the use of your flat. Due to a slight case of mistaken trust, I lost my uniform and so have borrowed a jacket and trousers from you. I shall return those on my arrival in Toronto. Yours, Wayne. I will call you up and tell you about it."

Grumet then showed him a suit jacket and a pair of trousers, not matched, which he identified as his. These were the clothes Lonergan had worn on his return trip to Canada that Sunday night. Grumet also showed him a box of Max Factor Pancake make-up, which Harjes identified as one he had found on the Tuesday after the murder, on a glass shelf in the downstairs washroom of his apartment. It was not, he said, his.

Grumet asked him if, when he returned Sunday night from his visit with friends, he had found anything in his desk. Harjes said he had found a plate of scrambled eggs and toast in the left-hand drawer. Then the prosecuting attorney showed him a dumbbell—Lonergan's alleged confession had stated that he had taken one of Harjes' dumbbells to weight his bloody uniform when he threw it into the East River—and he identified it as similar to ones he had owned. He had had four such dumbbells, he added; now he had three.

Grumet finished his examination, evidently satisfied. Broderick, cross-examining, began by asking Harjes if, in the four years he had known Wayne, he had found him "perfectly all right in all respects." When Grumet objected, Broderick rephrased it. "Did you ever hear anybody say anything bad about him?" Grumet objected, but Judge Wallace, although saying he didn't "think he [Harjes] is qualified on the reputation business, if that is the purport of that," allowed the question. Harjes said no, he never had heard anything "bad" about Lonergan.

Q. Now, Wayne Lonergan had, during the four years in which you knew him, been a guest of yours at different times, had he not?

A. No, not really.

Q. He hadn't been a guest at any time other than this particular time?

A. He stayed with me once.

Harjes then left the stand.

Detective William J. Wall, who worked as a stenographer in the Toronto Police Department, was called next. He had with him the stenographic notes of the questions put to Lonergan when the defendant was picked up in Canada, by Assistant District Attorney Loehr, and Lonergan's answers.

Judge Wallace, after looking over the statement, said it was his intention "only to admit that part that bears directly on what he was doing that night"—the night of the crime. "Otherwise," the Judge said, "there is a lot of stuff there about his preliminary maneuvers, about him claiming to be getting 4-F designation, all that sort of thing, making claim to homosexuality. I am going to keep that out at this time, unless you [Mr. Broderick] want the whole thing in. If you do, that is another matter, but that is my inclination at this time. I am doing it on the theory that it may be prejudicial to the defendant, a statement made that he got a 4-F classification, a claim he was a homosexual."

Wall began reading his statement. The session between Lonergan and Loehr took place, he said, in Toronto Police Headquarters in the presence of Detective Sergeant Arthur Harris and Wall himself.

Loehr: I suppose you know why you are being held. The investigation is about in its final status. Various witnesses have been investigated and the scene of the crime has been examined. The case is conclusive. Is there anything you want to tell us?

Lonergan: I cannot think of anything to say.

Loehr: Do you want to answer my questions?

Lonergan: I don't know.

Loehr: Are you willing to tell me the truth about this murder of your wife, Patricia?

Lonergan: Yes, but I don't know whether I should or not. I have been sitting around all day.

Loehr repeated his question. Lonergan said, "I am being charged with this murder, is that the idea?

Loehr: That is about it. You are going to have a chance to make a clean breast of it.
Lonergan: I might just as well wait.

Loehr asked him if he didn't want "to have a try" at answering the questions truthfully, to which Wayne replied that he was prepared to tell the truth "but it is a serious charge."

Loehr: Nothing could make you deviate from the truth?
Lonergan: I am very liable to say something stupid.
Loehr: I don't think you are a stupid young man and I am sure you will be able to avoid stupid answers.
Lonergan: I will answer your questions.

His name, he said, was Wayne Lonergan, and he was twenty-six years old. He had been born in Toronto and had lived there for twenty-one years. Before going into the RCAF, he stated, "I had lots of jobs but no special occupation." He attended St. Michael's School and Dominion Business College in Toronto, then went to New York City in 1939 and worked at the World's Fair, that year and the next. In the winters of those years, he added, he worked for Abercrombie and Fitch, the famous Madison Avenue sporting-goods store.

He had met Patricia Burton, Wall's statement continued, in 1939, having been introduced by her father, whom he had met previously. He married her in July of 1941, after having "more or less" kept company with her from 1939 to 1941. Billy Lonergan was born July 1, 1942, he said, and from the time of his marriage until the time of Billy's birth, he lived with Patsy continuously in New York. After the child was born, the Lonergans rented a little house in Stockbridge, Massachusetts, where they spent the summer, returning to 983 Park Avenue in New York in the autumn.

Loehr: Now, will you tell us the nature of your married life? Did it proceed smoothly?

Lonergan: Very smoothly, on the whole.

Loehr: No violent quarrels?

Lonergan: No.

Loehr: Just the ordinary differences between man and wife?

Lonergan: Yes.

Loehr: Nothing unusual?

Lonergan: No.

In the summer of 1943, Lonergan said, he and Patricia were separated. There was no single incident causing this; rather it was "a combination of things." "I became tired of going out during this summer," he added, "and I introduced her to this fellow who took her out all the time." "This fellow," he said, was Tim Krusi, attached to the American Field Service.

Loehr: Did her acquaintance with this man have anything to do with your disagreement with Patricia?

Lonergan: Well, yes, but I don't think it was particularly him. He was just there. It was general apathy on her part.

Loehr: Nothing specific?

Lonergan: No.

Loehr: What about the child? Did Patricia exhibit the usual motherly tendency toward the child?

Lonergan: Not particularly.

Loehr: Were you a normal father toward the child?

Lonergan: I don't suppose so.

The situation came to a head, Lonergan said, one week end when "she told me I would have to move out of the apartment, or she would move." He moved, he said, to Fire Island (an island off the shore of Long Island, which has acquired some reputation as a summer colony for homosexuals). He said he tried to bring about a reconciliation but Patsy "wanted to try living apart." Returning from Fire Island, he rented an apartment at 55 East

58th Street, with money provided by his wife. There, he said, he lived alone, although he saw Patricia several times.

Gabellini, he said, he had met "three or four years ago in some restaurant or other." He said he hadn't seen Gabellini in Patsy's company, but had heard she was going out with him. During this time of separation, he said, relations between Patsy and him were "very" amiable. He went out with other women, he added. On September 6 of that summer, he joined the Royal Canadian Air Force.

His visit to New York during the fateful week end, Lonergan went on, was his second leave. The week end before, he said, he also had been in Manhattan on a forty-eight hour pass, after having received a telegram saying that Patsy was in the hospital with appendicitis. Upon arriving, he had telephoned, and had found she wasn't in the hospital at all, and hadn't sent any wire; in fact, he never had found out who did send the wire.

Loehr: Then you went to see Patricia?
. .*Lonergan:* Yes.
Loehr: Slept with her?
Lonergan: Yes.
Loehr: Have relations with her, sexual intercourse?
Lonergan: Yes.

Then Lonergan told of his second week-end visit, of waking up Harjes and then staying in his apartment, of breakfasting with his host, and of calling a girl named Marcella D'Arnoux for lunch.

Newsmen scurried around to check on Marcella D'Arnoux. She was finally identified as a Hattie Carnegie saleswoman. She was also a French countess, a petite brunette of about thirty-five, who lived in a one-room apartment in back of a dress shop on East 60th Street, who said she had known Patsy Lonergan on the Riviera and "have known them both, here."

He lunched with Miss D'Arnoux at the Marguery Hotel, Lonergan went on, along with another girl, Sylvia French. Then he escorted Miss D'Arnoux back to Hattie

Carnegie's, after which he "took a walk along the street" with Miss French, as he hunted for a liquor shop. At a Fifth Avenue store he bought three small bottles of brandy and some Pernod for Miss French. She left him, and he watched a Navy parade along Fifth Avenue, after which he went to F. A. O. Schwartz, the Fifth Avenue toy store, and bought a toy elephant for fourteen dollars. This done, he took the elephant and went to Sylvia French's apartment on East 52nd Street, where "we had a couple of drinks of this French liquor."

Lonergan left Miss French's, he said, about five P.M., after having made no advances toward her, although he described her as "fairly" attractive. He left the elephant at her apartment, and took a cab back to Harjes' place. Harjes then introduced him to Jean Murphy Jaburg, who lived in the same building, and Lonergan asked her to attend *One Touch of Venus* with him, and, after she had broken another appointment, she agreed.

About six-fifteen he went over to Patsy's apartment. Miss Black let him in, and he went up to the nursery on the second floor. While there, he said, he went into Patsy's bedroom to call Harjes to see if Mrs. Jaburg had left any message. Then he called Mrs. Jaburg, and she confirmed the date, after which he returned to Harjes' apartment and had several drinks with her before they headed for the theatre.

By this time it was five P.M. in the courtroom, and Detective Wall seemed weary, and to be having a little trouble with his notes. Judge Wallace called a halt.

When the trial resumed on Friday, for the first time Wayne Lonergan seemed to show the strain. He looked haggard, worn, and nervous. He looked constantly around the almost empty courtroom, and drummed his fingers on the defense table.

The courtroom was almost empty, because Judge Wallace suddenly had ordered all spectators, except newsmen, barred. Only one man sat in the spectators' section; he was an elderly, gray-haired man and "was believed to be an official," according to news reports.

There was one small pretrial development this day. Word trickled in from Reno that Mrs. Alice Harjes, wife of John Harjes, had arrived at that city of divorce mills to establish residence for a parting of the ways. What grounds she would use had not been determined.

Detective Wall resumed reading the Lonergan statement made in Toronto. In it, Wayne said he and Jean Jaburg had gone directly to *One Touch of Venus* the night before the murder, without dining. He said he got along "all right" with Mrs. Jaburg, but was disappointed in the show.

After the theatre, Lonergan said, he and Jean had walked across town to the Waldorf-Astoria, but couldn't get into the Wedgwood Room. Then, he said, they had taxied to the Stork Club, but didn't stay there because— the Judge had to rap for order—there was "an abnormal crowd." Finally they landed at Twenty-One, where they ate and drank for an hour. The Blue Angel, incubator of show talent on East 55th Street, was the next stop. By this time it was one-forty-five A.M., and the show was just over. They stayed long enough for Lonergan, who had reported drinking previously at the Harjes apartment and then at Twenty-One, to have three more Scotches. They stayed at the Blue Angel until the place closed, just before three A.M.

Q. During this evening, did you talk about Patricia and your child to Jean?

A. I think so, yes. She asked me if I was married and I said yes. She told me she was married. I thought she had been divorced.

Q. What time did you leave the Blue Angel?

A. About closing time—about quarter to three.

Q. Where did you go then?

A. I took her home.

Q. Did you go into her apartment?

A. No.

Q. Are you sure of that or are you trying to be a gentleman?

A. I asked her into Harjes' apartment and we went in.

There, he went on, they had some Scotch and sodas. After that, he said, he took her "right home."

Q. Did you make any advances toward her?
A. No.
Q. She is a very attractive girl, is she not?
A. Yes.
Q. Did you go upstairs with her?
A. No.
Q. Did you kiss her then?
A. Yes.

Judge Wallace decided at this point that "we have had enough of that now. Get down to this last question: 'Did you have sexual intercourse with her in her apartment? Answer: No.' Go on from there," he ordered.

Lonergan then said he took Mrs. Jaburg to her apartment about four-thirty or five A.M., and returned to Harjes' apartment. To do this, he had to leave one entrance of the building and walk to another. It was during this walk, he said, "I picked up a soldier who was waiting on the corner." This would be "Murray Worcester."

Q. What did you say to him?
A. He said he was going downtown to get a room. I told him he would have a tough job that time of night. He said, "I will get one some way or other." Then I asked him in. I told him I had lots of room and an extra bed in my apartment.
Q. What did he say?
A. He said he would stay.
Q. Did you contemplate an act of perversion?
A. I vaguely thought about it.
Q. Did he go with you?
A. Yes.

Lonergan said, Detective Wall continued, that Worcester was a private first class in the "infantry, I imagine," and that the two of them went up to Harjes' apartment and had some Scotch.

Q. What did you do then?

A. We talked a while, and then went upstairs to bed.

Q. Did you each have a bed?

A. Yes.

Q. Did you stay in your bed?

A. No, after a while I climbed into the other bed with him.

Q. What did you do?

A. Nothing much—a few things.

Q. Acts of perversion?

A. Yes.

Q. Was the soldier willing?

A. Not too willing.

He went to sleep, Lonergan declared in his statement, about five-thirty or six A.M., awakening about ten or eleven A.M. He had a good breakfast of bacon and eggs and plenty of coffee, he went on, but the soldier didn't eat with him because he already had gone. Emil Petters, the butler, served the breakfast. The soldier, Wayne added, had taken his wrist watch and about a hundred dollars in cash, which he, Lonergan, had obtained by cashing a check.

Q. Did you tell Emil about losing your watch and money?

A. No.

Q. When did you discover your loss?

A. When I woke up.

Q. Didn't you hear the soldier leave?

A. No, I had taken some sleeping pills.

Q. Did you say anything when you woke up and found your watch and money gone?

A. To myself. I didn't say anything to Emil.

Q. What else was stolen?

A. My watch and money only. My wallet was there, plane ticket and identification card. My clothes were also stolen.

Q. Do you expect us to believe that?

A. I wouldn't.

Q. You are not serious?

A. I certainly am!

Lonergan said he had asked for a second helping of bacon and eggs from Emil, intending to feed the dog, but the dog wasn't there, so "I put it in the dresser. I didn't want the butler to think I was wasting his eggs and bacon," he added.

Later he dressed, went over to Sylvia French's apartment, picked up the toy elephant, and went over to Patsy's apartment. He got there about twelve-thirty P.M. Sunday, went in the front door, "and put the package inside about three feet." He returned to Harjes' apartment, and then he picked up Jean Jaburg for lunch.

Q. Is it not a fact that both you and your wife had been living abnormal lives, and abnormal things can happen, and there were, no doubt, some disagreements?

A. I have never had a violent disagreement at any time.

Q. Did you always take everything in a cold manner?

A. I suppose so.

Q. You felt very badly about your wife telling you to get out?

A. I don't know about that.

Q. But she had told you something that hurt you?

A. Yes.

Q. It is natural to assume that ever since this happened, it has been smoldering in your mind, it became an obsession and you wanted to get back on good terms with your wife?

A. I was on good terms with her.

Q. But you wanted to get back there, not only on friendly terms, but to the full status of man and wife?

A. I had no intention of doing that after I was in the Air Force and found I could not live a normal life.

Q. Did you have natural relationships with your wife?

A. Yes.

Q. Did you ever sicken your wife of it?

A. No.

Q. Did she ever refuse you?

A. Yes, a couple of times.

Q. Is it a fact that she refused you last Sunday morning, and this is what led to the trouble?

A. No.

Lonergan went on to say that he "realized there was not much point" in trying to reconcile with Patsy, and he admitted it was "very strange" that she was murdered on the day he happened to be in New York. "Nobody had a better reason for doing it than you," Loehr suggested, to which Wayne replied, "What is the motive?"

Loehr continued to hammer away with such questions as "Suppose I say you were seen to stay much longer [in Patsy's apartment on the morning of the murder]?" and "Why won't you tell us the truth?"

Lonergan then admitted he had known Dr. Michel for about two years, and had seen him the week before the murder.

Q. What did you say to him?

A. I asked him to sell me something.

Q. What was it?

A. Arsenic.

He said that he wanted the poison for "a party I knew," who would give him two hundred dollars a gram for it, and that he, Lonergan, had been prepared to pay Dr. Michel one hundred dollars. As for the "party," Lonergan said he didn't know the party's full name, or his reason for wanting the arsenic. He added that the doctor refused him, saying "it was enough to kill an army."

Q. This is what you were buying arsenic for—a complete stranger?

A. Yes.

Q. What did he want it for?

A. He would not tell me.

Q. Why were you so anxious to oblige a complete stranger?

A. I did not mind making a hundred dollars.

Q. This is a pretty farfetched story, and you know it is not the truth.

A. No, I do not know that.

Lonergan went on to say that he couldn't think of anyone who could have murdered his wife. He also said that he got no income from his acts of perversion; on the contrary, "it usually cost me money." Loehr returned to "Worcester."

Q. This man had a uniform; why did he want yours?

A. That is what I could not figure out.

Q. What particular acts of perversion did you commit with this man?

A. There are only two. Both of them.

Q. You did that before you were married?

A. Yes.

Q. Did you get much satisfaction out of living with your wife or any other woman?

A. Well, a certain amount.

Q. Did you ever make love to your wife in any other manner but by natural intercourse?

A. Yes.

Q. What was her reaction to this?

A. She did not like it and told me to do it somewhere else.

At about this point, Detective Sergeant Harris of Toronto had taken over the questioning from Loehr, and he asked several routine questions, after which the statement ended. Broderick waited a moment, until Detective Wall had stepped down, and then made his first move for a mistrial. He said he had been denied his true right to examine the Canadian statement on the question of admissibility prior to the admission of any such statement.

The motion was denied.

Elizabeth Black returned to the stand briefly, to testify that the apartment doors had been locked when the body was found. Loughram, the engineer in the district attorney's office, returned for similar testimony.

Next on the stand was Henry Vaccaro, a Teaneck, New Jersey, man who was a stenographer attached to the New York district attorney's office, and who previously had worked for Governor Thomas E. Dewey. It was Vaccaro that had taken down the alleged Lonergan confession, and it was this statement that Grumet now attempted to have the stenographer read.

Broderick began a desperate attempt to block the reading of the confession, at least at this time. First he said he wanted to examine the arresting officers in Canada "to show the chain of duress." But when he admitted he had not subpoenaed them, Judge Wallace brushed his motion aside. Broderick then made a surprise move. He called Grumet himself to the stand.

First Broderick inquired into his qualifications. Among Grumet's replies was one noting that he had been a member of Governor Dewey's famous special rackets investigation group, and later had served under Dewey in the district attorney's office. He proceeded to tell of the first time he saw Lonergan, when the suspect was brought into his office at dusk on October 27, 1943. Broderick asked Grumet about the layout of his offices, and Judge Wallace broke in to say that they were "large and sumptuous, Mr. Broderick."

"I have never been a public officeholder, Judge, and I would not know that," Broderick said.

The Judge sighed. "Well, that is too bad," he replied. "We have missed you."

Suddenly, the whole atmosphere resembled that of several weeks before, when the two attorneys were at each other's throats. Grumet testified that when Lonergan was brought to him that first day, detectives also brought along Wayne's bag containing "a couple of little bottles of cognac or brandy."

Broderick leaped to the attack.

"Didn't you feed Wayne Lonergan with this brandy all the time that you were questioning him in your room?" he barked.

"No," Grumet said. "That's not true, and you know it."

"What became of the brandy?"

"It may still be around, for all I know. Lonergan didn't drink it there."

Broderick picked up a photograph of the nude body of Patsy Lonergan, and waved it under Grumet's nose. "Did you flash People's Exhibit Five, the picture of his dead wife, or a duplicate of that picture, right under his nose, and say, 'You son-of-a-bitch, see what you did to your wife'?" he shouted at Grumet.

"I did nothing of the kind," the prosecutor replied heatedly. Judge Wallace broke in.

"Did you threaten the defendant at all, or use any threatening language?" he asked Grumet.

"I did not."

Grumet said that there "may have been as many as eight" detectives in the room at the time Lonergan was being questioned, but that he, Grumet, was the only one doing the questioning.

"Did you," Broderick exclaimed, "say to him, 'You son-of-a-bitch,' pointing your finger at him, 'I am going to put you in the electric chair and I am going to go up and laugh when I see them turn the juice on you'?"

"I did not."

Broderick then asked Grumet if Lonergan had been fed during that first night. Grumet said icily, "It is the usual practice in our office to feed witnesses." Lonergan, he added, was seated in a comfortable chair and did not complain of lack of sleep. The Assistant District Attorney said he finished questioning the suspect that night about four A.M., and then remained in his office and worked there until he went home at six-fifteen A.M. About ten A.M. he was back in the office, after having slept briefly at home. He did not know, he added, whether Lonergan had had any sleep in the interim before he saw him at two P.M. the next day, and said too that he had not directed anyone to provide sleeping facilities for the prisoner.

"At four-thirty P.M.," Broderick almost shouted, "did you telephone to the press room that 'we sweated him and broke him'?"

"That is ridiculous," Grumet snapped. He said he had nothing to do with the press, that that department was handled by his superior, Mr. Hogan.

After a brief recess, Broderick resumed hammering away at his legal opponent. He asked if Lonergan had asked "repeatedly" for his lawyer, Harry Civiletti, of the well-known firm of Alexander and Green at 42 Broadway. Grumet said no. Grumet then testified that before Lonergan had begun his alleged confession, he had told the same story he had given in Canada.

"He repeated it substantially," Grumet said, "the story that they engaged in acts of perversion, unnatural acts, that he performed an unnatural act for the soldier, and then he asked the soldier to do the same for him. The soldier was reluctant to do that, but finally agreed. He said that the soldier at one time refused to go on, and there was a tussle between them, and it was during that time that he said he received the scratches on his face.

"I believe I pointed out to him that the soldier would not be likely to scratch his face, that the likelihood is that would have been done by a woman and not a man—that a man would have probably punched him. He insisted that the soldier had made those scratches."

After lunch recess, Broderick, having finished his examination of Grumet, called John Loehr to the stand. The young assistant district attorney—who disclosed that he maintained residences in Yonkers, New York, and also at 20 Beekman Place, virtually next door to the Lonergans—told of interrogating Lonergan in Canada, and then described the interrupted journey with the suspect back to New York. At no time, he said, did anyone physically assault, beat, or strike Lonergan in his presence.

Loehr said that during the questioning in New York, he thought he had put two or three questions to the suspect, but that was all.

Q. Neither you nor any of the other men in the room said to Lonergan, "That goddamned homosexuality stuff won't look good in public print; you better come clean"?
A. I don't remember that.

Q. Did you see Captain Mahoney give him the palm treatment on the eye?

A. Nobody touched Lonergan.

It was during the New York questioning, Loehr went on, that he had shown to Lonergan the sections of the Penal Law dealing with cases of this sort. He said he had pointed out the differences between murder in the first and in the second degrees. "This," he added, "was when he had asked me about the definitions of the different degrees." He denied having made promises of any kind to Lonergan.

District Attorney Hogan came next to the stand. A sharp-minded, soft-spoken man, Hogan said that at no time had he authorized Loehr, or any other member of his staff, to promise Lonergan he wouldn't be prosecuted for murder in the first or second degrees. That was about the extent of his testimony, after which Judge Wallace, obviously worn from the bickering, adjourned court until Monday morning, "at which time I hope everybody will again be waiting for me."

Chapter Seven

IT WAS OBVIOUS, when the Monday, March 27, session in court began, that Broderick still was determined to pursue the vital issue of duress.

Wayne Lonergan looked alert and fresh. He had paper and a new, sharpened pencil on the table before him, and, as the early testimony began, he made several notes. There were two angry red marks, evidently cuts or scratches, on his right cheek, and his color was high. However, as the morning wore on, this flush receded from his rugged, handsome face, and he became quite pale once more.

The proceedings began with a parade of Canadian and New York policemen who had been involved in the arrest and questioning of the defendant. All denied duress.

Detective Sergeant Arthur Harris of Toronto was the first. Briefly he recounted his part in the week end's events, and then said that he had seen Lonergan, Loehr, and the two New York detectives off on the train for Manhattan. Lonergan reached for pencil and paper at this point, and scribbled what seemed to be a question, which he passed to his counsel. Broderick looked at it, then looked up at Sergeant Harris.

"Did you, sir," he said, "at any time between eight P.M. or eight A.M. Monday, October twenty-fifth, 1943, and eight P.M. Tuesday, October twenty-sixth, 1943, while the defendant was in the custody of the Toronto police, threaten to keep him in solitary confinement in the Dominion Jail unless he signed whatever papers you asked him to sign?"

Harris said no.

Detective Gordon Ferguson, another Canadian, followed Harris to the stand, but added little to Harris' story. Then the four policemen who had taken part in the lineup just before Lonergan confessed were put on the stand, one after another—Detectives James Riendeau, John G. Green, and

John McKeon, and Patrolman Thomas J. Quinn. Of Detective Riendeau, Broderick asked, "Did you hear Mr. Grumet in that room, either at the lineup or just before the lineup, say to the defendant, 'I will cook your hash with this lineup, so you better come clean'?"

"I never heard those words before," Riendeau replied. The other three policemen affirmed this answer. Broderick asked Quinn and McKeon if Grumet had brought a young lady into the room during the lineup. They said he had.

"Did she," Broderick asked McKeon, "at any time while you were in the lineup, put her hand upon Lonergan's shoulder, or any part of his body?"

Before the officer could reply, Judge Wallace excluded the question. "We are not on that subject now," he stated firmly.

Then came the morning's star witness, Detective William Prendergast of the East 51st Street station, who, with Detective Nicholas Looram, made the trip to Canada to bring Lonergan back to New York. As he testified on meeting Lonergan in Toronto and questioning him, Judge Wallace broke in and asked if the defendant had been threatened or abused by him or by anyone in his presence. "Never," Prendergast said.

The detective then told of the staggered journey back to New York, and of how the party of four—the two officers, Loehr, and Lonergan—had stayed overnight at the Hotel Statler in Buffalo. Lonergan, he said, got to sleep about five-thirty A.M., and awoke about eleven o'clock the same morning. The suspect, he said, ate a "hearty" meal of orange juice, oatmeal, either bacon or ham and eggs, rolls, and coffee.

In the face of Broderick's rapid-fire questioning, Prendergast made some denials. He denied that he had told Lonergan that he was being brought to New York for the funeral of his murdered wife. He denied he had promised Lonergan that he would be released in seventy-two hours. He denied that he or Looram "or anybody else" had accused Lonergan of homosexuality. He denied that Lonergan was handcuffed at any time, with the exception of that night in the Statler.

Q. Just prior to leaving the Hotel Statler in Buffalo, did some of the Buffalo police officers turn over to you two bottles of Johnny Walker Black Label Scotch, the long thin bottles, and say they were the best shape to carry when traveling on an airplane?

A. They did not give us any kind of liquor.

Q. On the way down in the airplane, did you give the defendant Lonergan liquor to drink, and tell him to be careful of the stewardess or steward because drinking liquor on the airplane was a violation of the federal rules covering airplane travel?

A. I never did that.

Q. When you took Lonergan out of the Toronto branch police station, did he have some liquor with him of any kind?

A. In his bag there were three bottles.

Q. Of what?

A. Brandy, which he purchased in New York, he said.

Q. Do you know what ultimately became of those bottles of brandy?

A. Yes, sir, I do.

Q. Was it twenty-year-old brandy?

Here Grumet interrupted to ask what difference that made, and the detective looked a little bewildered and said, "I don't know, frankly."

"Well," Judge Wallace put in, "what became of it, whether it was twenty-year-old or ten-year-old or five-year-old?"

"One was consumed on the train," the detective replied.

"Who had it?" the Judge asked.

"Lonergan had it," Prendergast said. "I had two drinks myself."

"Did Looram have one or two?"

"I believe Looram had two."

The bottle of brandy, the detective noted, was a half-pint one.

Broderick switched to another tack. "Now, in the Buffalo hotel, the Statler," he resumed, "did you and Looram say to Lonergan, 'You know it doesn't make much difference what you say about this murder case, because we have you hooked for sodomy, because you admitted you had unnatural relations and you can get twenty years for that, regardless of what happens to the murder case'?"

"We never discussed that, never discussed the case at all in that room," the detective answered.

Defense counsel brought the trip down to its terminus in Grumet's office. He asked Prendergast if Lonergan had a crew haircut. Prendergast said yes. "And did Captain Brennan put his hand on the top of his head and say, 'You will get a shorter haircut than that, up where we are going to burn you in the electric chair'?" Broderick asked. The detective said no.

Relentlessly Broderick pursued his man, trying to wrench an admission of duress from him. He had no luck.

Q. In that questioning period, he [Lonergan] was asked about the scratches on his face by one or more of the men questioning him, was he not?

A. He was asked by Mr. Grumet.

Q. And did Mr. Grumet say to him, "There is no use of your trying to deny the scratches, because we had scientific tests made of skin found under your wife's fingers"?

A. I don't recall him saying that.

Q. Did Lonergan say, "If you are going to start talking about skin, why don't you take samples of my skin and compare it with any skin that you have from under my wife's fingernails?"

A. He never said that.

Q. Did Lonergan, during that hour, say, "Why don't you give me a lie detector to find out who is telling the truth, me or you?"

A. Positively not.

Q. Now, at any time while you were in [Room] 608, did any of the police officers say to Lonergan, "Your father must be turning in his grave when he realizes that he married an insane woman and you turned out to be a————on him"?

A. No, sir. I don't know whether his mother was insane or not.

Slowly Broderick got around to Lonergan's disputed confession. He refused so to designate it; instead, he referred to it as a "statement" and an "examination," and he worked at length on Prendergast to discover if there were any legal discrepancies in the taking of the statement. He found none. Prendergast said that the statement took about three quarters of an hour, and that he did not recall Lonergan's signing the stenographer's notebook at the conclusion of the session.

Throughout the questioning, the slight, dark-haired detective had remained completely calm and cool. Broderick hadn't had the slightest luck in ruffling him. The lunch recess was taken.

In the press room, newsmen mulled over the events of the morning, and other developments that had cropped up unofficially. For the first time, the question of whether Wayne Lonergan, fighting for his life, would take the witness stand himself was considered.

In the beginning, it had been assumed more or less that he might. As the trial had worn on, however, the line of questioning by defense counsel had indicated that Broderick would try to save his man from the electric chair without producing Lonergan himself. Now, however, it developed that Lonergan had had a two-and-a-half-hour talk with Broderick in a Tombs cell the night before, after which Broderick had commented to one newsman that, under a Court of Appeals ruling in 1916 (the People vs. Trebis), a person could testify as to the truth or falsity of a statement attributed to him.

Over coffee and sandwiches, the crime reporters pondered this twist, but, just as the discussion was becoming heated, recess was over and they were called back to the courtroom.

Nicholas Looram, Prendergast's detective partner, was the first witness of the afternoon. He confirmed Prendergast's story about the brandy drunk on the train, and he added the information that Lonergan had been registered in the Buffalo hotel as "William Maloney" of "2oo some street" in New York, in order to avoid undue attention from "the newspaper people."

Captain Daniel J. Mahoney, commanding officer of the

Homicide Squad, next took the stand. Broderick went back to the angle of duress. "Did you, at any time that night [the night of Lonergan's preliminary questioning in New York], hit him a glancing blow with the palm of your hand on the eye area?" he demanded. Mahoney said no, and he flatly denied making the remark "Your old man must be turning in his grave."

Mahoney dismissed, Broderick announced that he had finished his questioning pertaining to the admission of the "so-called confession," and Henry Vaccaro, the stenographer, took the stand again, to begin reading the document. Before he could start, Broderick entered an objection to its being received in evidence, and Judge Wallace overruled him. Then Broderick asked that the reading be done directly from the stenographic notebook. Vaccaro picked it up, cleared his throat, and, in a flat, unemotional voice, began.

"Death of Patricia Lonergan," he read—and the words of Wayne Lonergan, spoken by a witness who seemed almost disinterested, began to fill General Sessions.

The statement had been made in question-and-answer form.

"Do you recall the events of October twenty-fourth, 1943, during the morning of that day?" Assistant District Attorney Loehr had asked.

"Yes," Lonergan had replied. Newsmen looked over at the defendant, but his expression had not changed.

Q. At about or in the morning of that day, did you go to the premises, 313 East 51st Street?
A. Yes.
Q. And what time did you arrive there?
A. About nine o'clock.
Q. Was it exactly at nine or shortly before?
A. A little before.
Q. How were you admitted to the premises?
A. I walked in and knocked on Mrs. Lonergan's bedroom door.
Q. And who admitted you when you knocked on Mrs. Lonergan's door?

A. Mrs. Lonergan.

Q. How was she dressed at the time?

A. She didn't have any clothes on.

Q. Had the bed been slept in?

A. Yes.

Q. Tell us how you talked and tell us what you said. Did you say anything to her about her recent behavior?

A. Yes, I got on to that.

Q. Will you tell us about that, please?

A. I said I had heard some mention of her hanging around night clubs all the time, and someone told me she was the belle of El Morocco, was there every night.

Q. Anything else you said to her about that?

A. I said she was behaving like a drunken sailor.

Q. What did she say?

A. "It is none of your business."

Q. Anything else that she said?

A. She said my behavior was not the best in the world, either—something to that effect.

Q. What did you say to that?

A. I asked her—I said she had been behaving like a tart.

Q. Will you tell us what names she called you?

A. A son-of-bitch and a dirty bastard.

Q. Did you reply to that?

A. I called her a couple of names, too.

Q. What names?

A. Again "tart."

Here, Lonergan's statement said, the conversation veered abruptly; Patsy asked him what "I was up so early for."

Q. What did you say?

A. I said, well, I understand she was going to the country and I wanted to see her before she left.

Q. When she asked you what you were going to do that day, what did you say?

A. I told her I was going to have lunch with a girl.

Q. Did she ask you who the girl was?

A. Yes.

Q. And did she ask you anything else?

A. She asked me what she was like.

Q. What did you say?

A. I said very pretty.

Q. And then what?

A. She got annoyed at that and asked, "Why don't you come to lunch with me?" I said I made a previous engagement and I couldn't break it.

Q. Did she say anything else about breaking the date or not breaking the date?

A. She got mad at me and she was visibly annoyed and she was furious about it.

Q. Did she *say* anything about being annoyed?

A. Yes.

Q. What was that?

A. She said she was annoyed that she didn't have control of every man.

Q. Tell us how this argument continued in your own words.

A. Well, I said she had never no right to feel that way; according to her, we were separated.

Q. Go on. I want you to tell it in your own words.

A. And then we just argued back and forth a little while. She started calling me names again for going out with this other girl.

Q. Did she ask you to leave?

A. Yes.

Q. Tell us about that.

A. She sat up in the bed, was mad, and pushed me and said, "Get out of here!"

Q. Was she in bed during all this conversation?

A. Yes.

Q. Where were you?

A. Sitting on the side of the bed.

Q. What happened when she pushed you away from the bed?

A. I got up and said, "If that is the way you feel about it—"

The courtroom now was very still as the stenographer

from the district attorney's office slowly, carefully—so undramatically as to be intensely dramatic—read on toward the violence of that gray and windy Sunday morning. When Patsy sat up in bed and pushed him, Lonergan went on, she yelled, "Get the hell out of here!"

Q. What did you do after you stood up?

A. I went over to the sideboard, the little table there where my hat and gloves were, and put them on.

Q. Tell us where that table is in relation to the bed.

A. Opposite the foot of the bed, on the other side of the room.

Q. Go ahead.

A. And she yelled at me, "Stay out of here! Don't ever come back! You will never see the baby again!"

Q. Did she call you— What happened then?

A. She told me this and I got mad.

Q. What did you do?

A. Picked up this candlestick right beside me and rushed over to her and hit her.

Q. Where did you hit her?

A. In the head. I think the side of the head.

Q. Which hand did you pick it up in?

A. My right hand.

Q. What did you do after you hit her on the head?

A. The candlestick broke and she sat up and said, "Good God, what have you done?"

Q. What did you do with the candlestick?

A. It broke to pieces.

Q. You dropped it?

A. Yes.

Q. What did you do then?

A. I was mad and I rushed over to the sideboard again and grabbed up another candlestick that was there.

Q. What did you do with it?

A. I hit her again.

When he hit her the second time, Lonergan said, she was still in bed, sitting up. After this second blow, she jumped out of bed, on the side opposite from him—the side near the window—and he raced around and "grabbed ahold of her."

Q. Did she say anything to you then?

A. She swore at me.

Q. Tell us what she said.

A. "You goddamned bastard!"

Q. And what did you do when you came up to her?

A. I grabbed ahold of her.

Q. Where?

A. Behind.

Q. Where?

A. Around the neck.

Q. Tell us what you did then.

A. I choked her.

Q. With both hands or one hand?

A. Both hands.

Q. For how long.

A. I don't know—it seemed to be long. Several minutes. About three minutes.

Q. Was she able to say anything else while you were doing that?

A. No.

So Patsy Burton had died. Lonergan stood there, and slowly realized that his wife was no longer moving. He stepped back. He was horrified, he said, "at this mess of blood all over the place."

Q. Where was she bleeding?

A. From her head, evidently.

Q. What did you do?

A. I started to go out.

Q. Yes—continue.

A. Then, suddenly, I realized I had blood all over my gloves and in front of my tunic.

Loehr switched the questioning back, for a moment, to the struggle itself, and asked Wayne if Patsy had defended herself. Yes, Wayne said—she had kicked, and she had scratched.

Q. Are those scratches which we see now on—two on the right side of your chin and two on the lower left side of your neck under your jaw and one near the tip of your left ear—were those scratches inflicted by your wife?

A. Yes.

Q. What did you do when you realized there was blood on your clothing?

A. I went to the bathroom to try and wash it off.

Q. Tell us how you did that.

A. I took a towel and wet it, and looked in the mirror, and saw those scratches on my face, and there was some blood on my chin, and I wiped it off with this wet towel, and I tried to wipe it off my tunic.

Q. Was the blood on your tunic from yourself or Mrs. Lonergan?

A. Mrs. Lonergan.

Q. What did you do then?

A. Then I left—left the house, put the towel in my pocket, the wet towel with the blood on it, and left the house.

Then, Lonergan said, he went "home"—or back to the Harjes apartment. To get there he walked—all the way up to the East Seventies, more than a mile. He got there about ten A.M. He saw many people on the way, he said, but none looked at his bloody uniform, so far as he knew. He stopped to talk with no one. He saw no one he knew. When he reached Harjes' apartment, he went upstairs and took a sedative, after which he removed the uniform.

Q. Tell us exactly in your own words every action that you made or took while you were upstairs in the bedroom.

A. I tried to clean off the uniform a bit with a towel, and it didn't work, and I got my duffel bag and tried to put it in there, but it wouldn't fit.

Q. What did you do after the uniform wouldn't fit?

A. I went downstairs and got a scissors.

Q. And what did you do?

A. Cut the uniform up.

Q. Then what?

A. Stuffed in into the duffel bag.

Q. Did you put anything else in the bag, other than the uniform?

A. My shirt and tie. Hat, gloves. A pair of socks.

Q. Can you think of anything else that you put in?

A. No. Before this I had put some money in there the night before, and I forgot about it.

Q. Anything else with the money?

A. I put my watch in there, too. Some blood was on the strap.

Q. Anything else that went in the bag?

A. Yes, I got a weight from downstairs.

Q. Will you tell us what that weight was?

A. A dumbbell—iron dumbbell.

It took Lonergan about half an hour to stuff all these items into the duffel bag, he went on. Then he washed and put on John Harjes' clothes, after which he rang for the butler and asked if breakfast was ready. It was, and he went downstairs to eat. The butler brought him scrambled eggs and bacon and orange juice.

Q. Tell us about your eating breakfast. Tell us exactly what you did.

A. I sat eating breakfast and I asked him if the Sunday paper was there and he gave me a Sunday paper.

Q. How much did you eat?

A. The orange juice and a piece of toast and a serving of bacon and eggs.

What was left of the food, he said, he placed on a small green plate he got from a nearby sideboard. This he took and put in the living room.

Q. Why did you take it into the living room?

A. I don't know.

Q. What did you expect to accomplish by that?

A. I did not know.

Q. Where in the living room did you place this dish containing the food?

A. I placed it on top of the desk—and changed it, put it inside the top drawer of the desk.

Slowly, surely, the portrait was drawn—the picture of a stunned, emotion-drained young airman, his wife lying dead in the luxurious bedroom a mile to the south, going through the motions of living as if in a dream. The dish of eggs in the desk, Lonergan turned and, still in a dream, went back into the dining room, where he had three cups of coffee. He drained most of the third cup, and then went upstairs and dressed for the street. By this time it was eleven-two A.M., Lonergan said.

Q. What did you do after you finished dressing?
A. I went and took the duffel bag and walked out of the house.
Q. Where did you go?
A. Along 79th Street.
Q. In which direction, east or west?
A. East.
Q. How far east did you go?
A. To the river [the East River].
Q. What did you do when you got to the river?
A. Threw the duffel bag in.
Q. What happened to the duffel bag after you threw it in the river?
A. It floated down the stream.
Q. How far into the river did you throw it?
A. Just a few feet. About five feet.
Q. Where did you go after you turned away?
A. Back west.

Now, with at least some of the evidence washed away, Lonergan took a deep breath and walked downtown a couple of blocks to 74th Street and Second Avenue.

Q. What did you do when you got to 75th or 74th Street?
A. I remembered my scratches and I looked for a drugstore.

Q. What did you get in the drugstore?
A. Max Factor Pancake make-up.
Q. Where did you go after that?
A. Harjes' apartment.
Q. Did you make any stops on your way?
A. No.

By this time, Lonergan said, it must have been fifteen minutes before noon. He saw Harjes' maid, and asked her for a glass of beer, which he took into the living room and drank. Then he asked her where he could find a newsstand, and she told him there was one around the corner. He went out to the stand and bought a *News* and a *Mirror,* the New York City tabloids. He asked for some magazines that the keeper of the stand did not have, and then went to another stand down the street, but that place didn't have the magazines either. Lonergan then returned to the apartment, finished the half-full glass of beer, and telephoned Sylvia French. He wanted to get the toy elephant he had left at her apartment, he said.

Q. What conversation did you have with Sylvia French on the phone?
A. I asked her if I could come down and get the toy, and three bottles of brandy, which I had purchased the day before.
Q. What did she say?
A. She said, "I am not up yet—give me half an hour."
Wayne agreed and hung up. Then he picked up the phone again and dialed Jean Murphy Jaburg.
Back on Beekman Hill, Billy Lonergan and his nurse had left the apartment, and there was only one occupant left. *Rigor mortis* was slowly setting in as Patsy Lonergan's husband got ready to take another woman to lunch.
Mrs. Jaburg accepted Lonergan's luncheon invitation, although she was still in bed. Lonergan said he would call her after one P.M. to see if she was up yet.

Q. Did you make any other telephone calls?
A. No.

Q. How long did you wait in the apartment after finishing that second call?

A. About twenty-five minutes.

Q. What did you do then?

A. I took a taxicab.

Q. Where did you go in the cab?

A. The Plaza Hotel.

Q. What did you do at the Plaza Hotel?

A. Cashed a check.

Q. For how much?

A. Twenty-five dollars.

He had kept the cabbie waiting while he went into the hotel to cash the check; he came out again and directed the driver to Sylvia French's apartment. When he got there, he told her how sorry he was to have missed her the night before, how he had run into some friends, and he picked up his toy elephant and the bottles of brandy. He was there only a few minutes, while the same cab waited. When he emerged from the building, he told the hackie to take him to Patsy Burton Lonergan's apartment.

Q. What did you do when you got to Mrs. Lonergan's apartment?

A. I left the toy.

Q. Will you tell us exactly how you did that?

A. I took the toy up the brownstone steps and left it in the hall.

Q. Exactly where in the hall did you leave it?

A. Inside of the door.

Q. Did you see anyone in the hallway?

A. No.

This strange mission accomplished, Lonergan drove back to the Harjes apartment. It was now about twelve-forty-five, and he telephoned Jean Jaburg. She was up and ready, and she told him that she planned to have her son lunch with them. Wayne said that would be all right, and in a couple of minutes he went to her apartment, arriving about one P.M.

It was five minutes to five by the clock in General Sessions. Judge Wallace quietly interrupted Vaccaro in his reading, and said that that would be about enough at this time. He went through his usual routine of telling the jurors not to discuss the case or form any opinion of guilt or innocence, and then he adjourned the case for the day. The faint overtones of dusk began to settle over New York City. Wayne Lonergan, much paler than he had been when the long day had begun, followed his attendants out of the courtroom and back to his cell in the Tombs. There was a strange quiet over the emptying room. No one had much to say.

Chapter Eight

THERE WERE FORTY-THREE PAGES to the "confession, so called," as Broderick had put it, by Wayne Lonergan. Most of it had been read that Monday. When court resumed Thursday morning, the bespectacled Vaccaro had only a little more to read—but in that little was a small bombshell. Lonergan said flatly that he had tried to kill himself long before he murdered his wife.

Loehr had been doing most of the questioning, in the taking of the confession. Then Grumet had taken over, asking the suspect if he had made any recent effort to buy arsenic. Lonergan said he had—that he had gone to two drugstores in Toronto, and then to "Dr. Michel in New York" about a week or two before being taken into custody. He said the story he had told to Dr. Michel, of seeking it for a friend, was not the truth.

"You really wanted it yourself, didn't you?" Grumet fired at him.

"Yes."

"For what purpose did you want it?"

"For the purpose of suicide."

"You're sure you didn't want it to give your wife?"

"Yes," Lonergan replied.

Vaccaro read on. The statement revealed that Lonergan also had tried to obtain strychnine, without success.

"Did you ever attempt suicide?" Grumet asked.

"Yes," Lonergan said.

"When?"

"Over a year ago."

"But you didn't succeed?"

"No."

"Why?"

"I backed out, the last minute."

"You got cold feet?"

"Yes."

104

There was a little more to the confession, so called; Lonergan disclosed that shortly after their marriage his wife had named him sole beneficiary in her will—but two months before the murder she had disinherited him. Her personal wealth, Wayne added, was about $230,000, but she would receive some seven million on her grandmother's death. Also, he put in, she gave him about seven hundred dollars monthly to pay household and personal bills.

Lonergan, unshaven this day, seemed bored as Vaccaro finished reading. There was a brief examination of the witness by both Grumet and Broderick, and then he stepped down. The Lonergan confession was on the record.

Jean Murphy Jaburg took the stand. She was pretty, almost striking, in a blue suit with a soft purple felt hat turned up in front to show her curled blonde hair, and wearing green gloves and carrying a matching green bag. She told the court she lived at 164 Sunset Avenue in Palm Beach, Florida, and sat back, relaxed and smiling, to answer Grumet's questions. Lonergan stared coolly in front of him. There was no sign that he recognized the bit actress and musical-comedy performer he had taken out on the Saturday night before the murder, and then the next day had taken to lunch at the Plaza Hotel.

Briefly she corroborated the story of their Saturday night together. She told of meeting Wayne for the first time at six P.M. and then of being taken home and left by Lonergan about three-forty-five A.M. Judge Wallace addressed her.

"The time you left him," he asked, "was he drunk or sober?"

"He was neither."

"What do you mean by that? He had had a few drinks?"

"Yes."

"Well," the Judge said, a little impatiently, "was he able to walk, talk—knew what he was saying and everything?"

"Apparently," Mrs. Jaburg said calmly.

After lunch at the Plaza, Lonergan took her home, stayed about ten minutes, and then left, she said. That, she added, was the last time she saw him, until this morning in the courtroom.

Q. Now, when you went out with him on Saturday night as you have described, what sort of clothes was he wearing?

A. His uniform.

Q. And when you met him again on Sunday, how was he dressed?

A. He had on a gray suit; the trousers and coat did not match.

She asked him about his uniform, she testified, and at that point, instead of replying, he asked her for a bottle of beer. She brought him, instead, some Scotch and soda, and repeated her question—"and he told me the story that he had met a soldier and befriended him and asked him to spend the night in Mr. Harjes' apartment, and when he waked the soldier had gone and taken his uniform and his money and his watch." She said she asked him why he didn't call the police.

"What did he say?" Grumet asked.

"He said he would." There was, she added, "nothing apparently" different in Lonergan's manner on Sunday as compared with his manner on Saturday.

Cross-examining, Broderick asked Jean about her marital status. "Do I have to answer that?" she asked. Ultimately, she said she was legally separated. Nothing further was asked along those lines. When she stepped down from the stand at the end of her testimony, she turned toward Lonergan, who had been languid in appearance, and smiled at him. He gave no sign of recognition.

Max Levinson took the stand next. It was into Levinson's drugstore, at 1440 First Avenue, between 74th and 75th Streets, that Lonergan reportedly had gone on the fatal Sunday morning to buy the make-up for his scratches.

Levinson recalled the morning. He recalled the man coming in about eleven thirty A.M. to buy the make-up. He recalled his appearance. He was, he said, tall "and he didn't comb his hair; his hair was just curled like, it wasn't combed back or side. It just had little indentations."

"Will you look around the courtroom and see if you can recognize that person?" Grumet asked. When Levinson said he could, Grumet requested him to "come down and put your hand on his shoulder."

The druggest walked unhesitatingly to the defense table and pointed squarely at Lonergan.

For a moment there was a hush in the courtroom. But Wayne Lonergan simply sat there, staring ahead. If he had shown no interest in Jean Murphy Jaburg, and he showed even less in Levinson. He simply sat there and stroked his unshaven chin, slowly, idly, with his right hand.

When Broderick started cross-examining the druggist, there came the first definite indications that his case was coming apart at the seams. He seemed to grope. Some of the questions he put to Levinson had no apparent bearing on the case at all. ("And what are the dimensions of your store?")

Ultimately, he did wring one admission from Levinson— that the druggist had not noticed any scratches on Lonergan's face when the defendant came into the store to buy the make-up.

Chiseling away, Broderick also won the admission that the box of Max Factor make-up introduced into the proceedings as a people's exhibit was not necessarily the one that had been sold to Lonergan. "You cannot say of your own knowledge," he asked Levinson, "that that is the box that you sold to the defendant, can you?" Levinson said it was the same color. "But that box and its contents," Broderick pursued—"you cannot say that that is what you sold to the defendant?"

"No," the druggist said.

Annalise Schonberg took the stand. A plain, brown-haired woman, wearing a black suit and a white blouse, she said she was employed as a nurse by Mrs. Franklin Ray, Jr., the occupant of the duplex apartment situated directly over the Lonergan flat.

Grumet asked Miss Schonberg if she recalled doing anything unusual on the morning of Sunday, October 24, 1943, and she said yes.

Q. All right, now, tell us just what you did.

A. Well, I was taking care of a scarlet-fever patient on the fourth floor, and I had finished his breakfast and was taking the dishes down to the third floor to sterilize when the child had asked me to pick up the morning papers for him several times.

Q. The child?

A. The child I was taking care of.

Q. Yes—keep your voice up.

A. And I washed the dishes and put them into the sterilizer, and then I opened the butler's pantry door, and as I opened it I heard screams, and I continued from the butler's pantry down to—

Q. You heard screams; you were in the butler's pantry; is that right?

A. That's correct.

Q. Do you know whether or not they were the screams of a woman?

A. They were.

Q. What sort of screams were they?

A. Well—

Broderick: I object to it, if the court pleases.

Judge Wallace: Can you give us an imitation?

Q. Yes—can you?

A. No, I am sorry, I cannot. They were quite loud, shrill.

Miss Schonberg said she then proceeded down two flights of stairs to the head of the stoop, where she picked up the morning papers. Then she went back up.

"Just a minute," Grumet put in. "At any time while you were going down those two flights of stairs did you hear anything else?"

"Yes. I heard a woman say, 'What are you doing? Stop that!' And at one point, 'Oh, my—blank.' I did not catch the rest of that."

When Annalise Schonberg came back upstairs with the Sunday papers, she paused outside Patsy Lonergan's door. "I raised my hand to knock," she said, "and then I thought better of it." She added that she had heard several more screams on her way up to the Lonergan landing from the stoop below.

While she stood at the door, she said, she heard "just— I don't know—sort of a little scuffling or something, nothing very loud, outside of the voice."

Q. What did you do after that?

A. Well, I returned upstairs. Walked up to the third floor.

Q. Yes?

A. And I went and I sat. I went through the butler's pantry into my room, which is right directly above Mrs. Lonergan's, and I started to look at the morning paper, and as I did so, I had finished about, I would say, half a page or one page of the comics, and I heard two very shrill, loud screams, and I rushed to the landing and leaned over and I could not hear anything after that. I went back to my room and I sat there for about twenty minutes, and then went back upstairs, and I did not hear anything after that.

When Broderick questioned Miss Schonberg, he asked where Mrs. Ray was while all this was going on. The nurse said that she was asleep.

Judge Wallace interrupted. "Did you say anything to her about hearing these screams?" he asked.

"No. I only saw Mrs. Ray for two minutes that entire day."

"Why didn't you call up the police or somebody, if you thought there was something wrong going on there?"

"Well," the nurse replied, "I knew that Mrs. Lonergan had help, and I thought that if they didn't interfere, it wasn't my place to do so."

Detective Looram and Inspector Kenny then took the stand again briefly, for short questions about the make-up and the dumbbell, and Judge Wallace called a recess. After lunch the trial resumed—with a mildly comic interlude. Before the jury trooped in, Judge Wallace addressed the counsel.

"The foreman of the jury just spoke to me," he announced. "He says that something appeared in the newspaper, a little squib in one of those gossip columns, to the effect that one of the jurors is having trouble with his wife and she was telling everybody he was a this and that.

"The foreman said he thought that it might be his wife. He said his wife had been around night clubs at times, came home the other night and there was a little dispute between them, and she may have been the one that is calling up the paper."

The Judge smiled a little. "I said, 'Do you think that would in any way interfere with your judgment on this case? If you feel that anything that has happened in this regard might affect your judgment as a juror, might embarrass you in the rendition of a verdict, tell me so.' He said, 'I don't think it would.' "

This noted, Broderick asked for a couple of minutes with his colleagues in another room to talk over the matter; then he returned and said that the foreman was a satisfactory juror to the defense.

The sixteenth witness for the state, as the afternoon session began that Tuesday, was Ruth Foster, an attractive young girl dressed in a white blouse with lace collar and cuffs and a small velours hat with blue lace. Miss Forster was the daughter of a woman who ran a florist shop at 143 East 79th Street. On that grim Sunday morning, she testified, she left the shop about eleven A.M. to go for a walk with her dachshund.

When she emerged into the street, she testified, she saw Lonergan—whom she had known for more than a year before that day, having met him at a cocktail party in Harjes' apartment—coming out of 140 East 79th Street, the Harjes apartment house. "I noticed he was carrying a dark blue bag—they call it a duffel bag, I guess. At first he was dragging it, then he threw it heavily over his left shoulder and headed east toward Third Avenue."

The next time she saw Wayne Lonergan was "the night that I was down at the district attorney's office—the night that he came back from Canada, I believe."

After a few inconsequential questions by Broderick, Ruth Forster stepped down. There was a momentary lull.

Grumet got to his feet. "The people rest," he said. The

black-and-gilt clock in the courtroom said three-fifteen.

Judge Wallace sent the jury temporarily out of the room "while I listen to motions by counsel for the defense, with which you have no concern." Even the jurors, however, unskilled as they were in the law, might have anticipated what at least one of these motions would be. Broderick made this one first.

"If it please the court," he said, "the defense respectfully moves the dismissal of this indictment on the ground that the people have failed by credible and believable testimony to connect the defendant with the commission of the crime charged."

He would have been less than a good attorney for his client if he had not made the motion.

"Motion denied."

"Exception," Broderick said, just as matter-of-factly as the Judge. "The defense respectfully requests Your Honor to withdraw from the jury the consideration of murder in the first degree."

"Motion denied."

There were three more such motions, covering murder in the second degree and manslaughter in the first and second degrees. When Broderick had taken his exceptions, Judge Wallace ordered another ten-minute recess, and then brought the jury back in. The Judge peered over the bench at Broderick. "Proceed," he said.

The portly lawyer got to his feet. "Mr. Gabellini," he called. There was no answer. Several calls by a court attendant produced no Mario Gabellini.

"Where is he, Mr. Grumet?" the Judge asked.

Grumet shrugged. "I was just told about it before we went out to lunch," he replied.

"Well, call somebody else," the Judge said.

Broderick protested. "Could we adjourn until tomorrow morning?" he asked plaintively. "It will interfere with the strategy of my case. I use strategy in the professional sense."

The Judge shook his head. "I think we will be able to get the import of the case if we call one man out of turn. Go ahead."

Broderick then called Dr. Michel. No answer.

Judge Wallace eyed Broderick speculatively. "Have you subpoenaed any of these people?" he asked.

"Why," the defense counsel said in an injured tone, "I understood that he would have them here."

"You understood nothing," Grumet retorted. "He never even mentioned it."

The Judge addressed Broderick. "You could have subpoenaed any and all these witnesses," he pointed out.

Broderick seemed to sulk. "The District Attorney misled me," he said. He then recalled to the stand, as the first witness for the defense, Detective William Prendergast. Broderick held up to him a yellow rubber garment that had been in Lonergan's suitcase on the trip from Canada to New York. It had previously been labeled by newspapers and police as "a yellow girdle."

"That is a bathing trunk, isn't it, rather than a girdle?" Broderick asked, dangling the item before the detective.

Prendergast peered, confused. "I don't know what that is, to tell you the truth."

Then slowly Broderick led the detective through a recounting of the events of that Sunday night when Patsy Lonergan's body was found, and of the detective's own part in it. When Grumet objected to one of these questions, which seemed irrelevant, Broderick turned to Judge Wallace, and for a moment it appeared as if he were going to begin one of the diatribes with which he had studded the earlier sessions presided over by Judge Freschi.

"Judge," he said sonorously, "this is the first time in history—"

That was as far as he got.

"No speeches," the Judge said dourly. "We don't care anything about history here. We are looking into the question of the guilt or innocence of this defendant and nothing else." Broderick said that he was just trying to find the facts. "Get on with it," the Judge said. Broderick took exception to that.

"I want no more talk about it," Judge Wallace said decisively.

There was very little talk about anything that day. When

evening adjournment came, the defense had made something less than an auspicious beginning.

Wednesday, March 29, was not to be just another day in the trial of Wayne Lonergan. It was to shock onlookers out of their seats, but there was no premonition of this as the proceedings began.

Before any defense witness took the stand, Broderick tried to have accepted as evidence a report from the hospital in Toronto where Lonergan's mother was said to have been confined on several occasions before she died. Grumet objected, on the grounds that there had been no foundation laid for the report. Judge Wallace sustained the objection, but finally allowed the report to be marked for identification.

"Do I understand," the Judge said to Broderick carefully, "that you are interposing the defense that the defendant, if he committed this act, at the time he committed it was insane—that he did not know the nature and quality of his act or that it was wrong? Is that your contention?"

"At this time, if it please the court," the attorney answered, "I would not like to disclose the defense further than the offer I made."

Isidore Michel, a doctor with offices on the upper East Side, was the first morning witness. He said he had known Patsy Lonergan since March 1942, when she first came under his care, and Wayne Lonergan since the same time. That was about all Broderick elicited from him on examination.

Grumet had more in mind, as he cross-examined. He asked Dr. Michel about the call that Lonergan made to his offices on October 23, 1943.

Q. Tell us what he said to you and what you said to him.

A. He announced himself through the secretary and, as he was in a Canadian uniform, the secretary announced, "There is a Canadian soldier, this and this name" and he would like to see me for a few minutes. I asked him to come in. I was quite busy and he says he does not want to see me professionally but he would like to get some medicine from me. I said, "What is the nature of the medicine?" He says he wants to get arsenic. Since I was busy, I told him to come back, and I would talk to him about five o'clock in the afternoon.

Q. Yes—did he come back?

A. He came back at five o'clock in the afternoon, and I asked him what he wants arsenic for, and he told me he wants one gram of arsenic. I said, "What do you want it for?" He says he wants it to send to a soldier outside of this country—that he got one hundred and fifty dollars and he would pay me a hundred dollars to give him one gram of arsenic. I told him that "it is too bad," I said, "that you got the money, but the arsenic that you ask for is poisonous and could poison a lot of people." I said, "Do you know what he wanted the arsenic for?"

Q. Referring to the soldier?

A. The soldier. He says, "Well, I presume he wanted to commit suicide." I said, "Knowing so, would you give him the arsenic, send him the arsenic?" He said, "Yes." I said, "Wouldn't your conscience bother you?" He says, "No—everybody is allowed to do with their lives what they please." I said, "Would you want me to be a party to anything like this?" He says, "Nobody need know about it." And I told him, "I am sorry, that is out of the question."

Here, Dr. Michel testified, Lonergan said, "It is too bad, I have already spent fifty dollars out of the hundred and fifty dollars and I cannot replace it."

"He says, 'Could you give me strychnine?' " Dr. Michel said. "I says, 'Strychnine is the same poisonous drug.' Then we simply spoke about flying, and I told him that he is lucky that he is in the flying corps—it is better than to be on the ground as a soldier—and he disagreed with me and said that the mortality of the flyers is ten per cent. That is, they had ten per cent chance of coming back alive.

"And he left."

Mario Gabellini was the next witness. Elegant in a brown suit, handsome and dark, he gave his full name as

Mario Enzo Gabellini, said that he had been born in Rome, had come to this country fifteen years ago, had twice been divorced, and dealt "chiefly in antique decorations."

Calmly he said he had met Patsy Lonergan "two or three years ago at a benefit ball for the British Relief Society." In three years or so, he added, he "met her occasionally at parties or hotel parties." He said that he had met Wayne Lonergan at a Christmas Eve cocktail party in 1942.

Broderick tried to paint a picture of Gabellini as something of a gigolo, asking him if he had been a professional dancer at one time, and if Patsy had given him ten dollars with which to pay the cab fare on their last evening together. Gabellini entered denials; he denied, too, that he had a key to the Yale lock on Patsy's bedroom door.

He told of the dinner that night at Louise's, on East 58th Street.

Q. Now, you say that you and Mrs. Lonergan used about three hours at dinner?

A. Yes.

Q. Did Mrs. Lonergan have something to drink during those three hours?

A. We had a cocktail. Then we met some friends and we all got together—you know.

Q. How many drinks would you say Mrs. Lonergan had during those three hours at Louise's?

Judge Wallace interrupted. "What is the materiality of that?" he inquired.

Broderick turned to him dramatically. "It is the contention of the defense that Mrs. Lonergan was very, very drunk, Judge."

Gabellini continued his story; he and Patsy had had "one, two, three" drinks, possibly, and some wine at dinner. From there they had gone in a party, with Farrell and Mrs. Farrell, to the Stork Club.

"Did there come a time when the management of the Stork Club asked Mrs. Lonergan to leave because she was highly intoxicated?" Broderick demanded.

"No," the witness replied. "Not at all, sir."

From the Stork, he continued, they went to the Farrell apartment in the Peter Cooper Hotel on East 39th Street, where they stayed "quite a little time, talking around." At six A.M., he said, they left and went over to Patsy's apartment.

In response to Broderick's question, Gabellini said that he had been to the Lonergan apartment "about ten times, something like that." Then he testified that on the Thursday evening before, there had been a party in the Lonergans' apartment, after which he and Patsy and six other persons went dancing at El Morocco. It was there, he added, that Patsy met Captain Elser.

Q. Did you and Mrs. Lonergan quarrel repeatedly about her attention to Captain Elser?

A. No, sir. I was resenting the manner.

Q. You were what?

A. I was resenting the manner of the Captain, because I met him on the dancing floor, and he was dancing with a girl and we were introduced. Then he went to take the girl to her place, and come back and calling me and I said, "Why do we exchange partners?" I say, "It is much easier to leave her standing." He said, "This is the American custom. You better go sit down; I better go back to the table," and he asked her to dance, that is all; didn't have any arguments or fight. I didn't have any right to.

Q. When you quarreled with Mrs. Lonergan because of your resentment at Captain Elser, did Mrs. Lonergan say, "Why"—speaking to you—"you are only a guinea pimp. The five hundred dollars a month I have been paying you for the last year, I have cut it off?

A. Please, Jesus.

Switching back to the Saturday-night date, Gabellini said that after he took Patsy home, about six-fifteen A.M., he went to a little food shop near his own apartment and had some breakfast. He brought the cab driver into the shop with him, he added. Broderick asked if he had brought the hackie into the shop to "tell him to say nothing about a fight that you and Mrs. Lonergan had in front of her house at Three-thirteen East Fifty-first Street about Captain Elser?"

"Of course not," Gabellini replied.

And, without any marked success in his attack, Broderick terminated the questioning of the decorator. Grumet tossed in one final query; he asked if Mrs. Lonergan had been drunk when Gabellini took her home. The answer was no.

There was a brief recess, during which the jury left the room. When the jurors filed back in, they were polled, after which Judge Wallace looked over at Broderick.

"Proceed," he said. Broderick got to his feet and started toward the bench. Then he turned and walked back to the defense table, where Wayne Lonergan sat as impassively as ever. The attorney bent toward the defendant and whispered.

As Broderick spoke, Lonergan nodded. Then, after a moment, he put out his hands in a gesture that seemed to indicate, "I don't care." Broderick straightened up and looked up at the Judge. It was eleven-fourteen A.M.

"The defense rests," he said.

After calling only three witnesses, the defense had rested. There were about fifty newspapermen, comprising almost the entire spectator audience, in the courtroom. Now, with a great surge, they swept toward the exit doors, waving papers, talking loudly, and aiming, of course, for the telephones.

Technically, the testimony-taking part of Wayne Lonergan's trial was not done; there still remained the calling of any rebuttal witnesses before the two attorneys went into their summations. But, for all practical purposes, Edward V. Broderick had done all he could for his client.

Wayne Lonergan sat at the defense table, as unmoved as ever. His counsel had shut off any avenue by which he could testify, since the prosecution was not allowed by law to call him.

He looked as if he didn't have a care in the world.

There was some unfinished business to clear up, incidentals to round out the trial. Broderick, who had been trying to show that Lonergan's duffel bag could not have reached the muddy East River waters if he had thrown it from the spot the prosecution declared he had, attempted to persuade Judge Wallace to order the jury to inspect that part of the water front for itself.

The Judge said he didn't feel that was necessary. Grumet helped out by calling Larry Froeber, a *Daily News* photographer, to the stand, and asked him to identify a photograph that he had taken of the disputed area. He did. Judge Wallace then said he would admit the photograph as evidence, if a witness was produced to say that that was the spot in which Lonergan said he had stood when he tossed the bag. Acting Captain Mahoney was recalled to the stand for that purpose, and the photograph was admitted.

After lunch, Grumet called Felix Guiffer, a Brooklyn cab driver, to the stand. Guiffer, it appeared, was the man who had driven Gabellini and Mrs. Lonergan to her apartment, and who later had had a cup of coffee with Mario.

The driver apparently backed up Gabellini's alibi. When Judge Wallace interrupted the questioning to ask how long Gabellini had taken to see Patsy to her apartment door, Guiffer said, "He just had enough time to go up the stairs and come down again."

Gabellini, he said, seemed "perfectly sober," and Patsy Lonergan "seemed to look all right to me."

There were no further witnesses. Judge Wallace then took up the matter of Dr. Michel's testimony. He said he was going to have it stricken from the record "on the ground that if the defendant had such a conversation with him and *did* attempt to purchase arsenic, that that is too remote from the occurrence in this case to warrant the jury finding any inference unfavorable to the defendant from that attempted purchase.

"In other words," he said, "there are too many different inferences that could be drawn from the attempted purchase, if it was made, and it would be dangerous for the jury to find that the defendant attempted to purchase arsenic for the purpose of, perhaps, using it to poison his wife."

As for Lonergan's testimony, through the statements introduced by the prosecution, "it is merely allowed to stand on the questions as to whether or not at that time he was making a free and voluntary statement concerning other events of which that [the reported attempt to buy the poison] was a component part.

"Now," he added, "is there anything else?"

Broderick arose. "If it please the court," he said, "the defense respectfully requests the dismissal of this indictment on the ground that the people have failed by creditable and believable testimony to establish any criminal connection of the defendant with the crime charged."

"Motion denied," Judge Wallace said.

The jurors were sent out of the room.

The Judge turned to the defense counsel. "Mr. Broderick, this morning you made an offer here in evidence of the report of somebody in Toronto, whatever it was. I asked you whether or not you were on the theory that the defendant at the time of the commission of this crime, if he did commit it, was insane. In other words, whether you were going to use that as a basis for interposing an insanity defense in order that I might rule on it. At that time you said, 'At this time, if it please the court, I would not like to disclose the defense further than the offer I made.' "

Judge Wallace peered closely at Broderick.

"Now," he went on, "I take it that you, as an officer of this court, at this time have no desire to deceive the court as to what your future intentions are, and I ask you now whether you made this offer of this alleged insanity commission for the purpose of interposing a defense of insanity for this defendant?"

"I made it in good faith," the lawyer replied, "because I did not know just how far we would go with the case. I did not decide until you gave me that five- or ten-minute recess just what my final decision would be on the case."

"You see," the Judge said with a sigh, "it is very difficult for me to fathom what is in your mind, because I know that you had an order for a psychiatrist to examine this defendant. I am informed he did so examine him on two occasions. And if it was your intention to interpose a defense of insanity, these interrogatories might become pertinent and relevant—and if you tell me that is so, why, then I will consider the question of admitting them in evidence." He shrugged. "But to just throw them in with nothing does not seem to me to mean anything."

"I am not offering any further testimony in this case of any nature whatsoever," Broderick replied.

"May I ask," the Judge said, "if the defendant is satisfied? Is he satisfied with that situation? After all, he is the one on trial here."

"That is true, Judge," Broderick said. "I kept that in mind from the beginning of the case."

"They may acquit him," the Judge went on. "They may convict him of manslaughter. I don't know. But, having in mind the seriousness of the charge, I want to give the defendant and you every opportunity to interpose any defense you want to interpose."

Broderick shook his head. "I am resting my case completely at this time, Judge," he said.

Judge Wallace called the jurors back in, and said the case was being adjourned until ten A.M. the next day. The gavel was banged. Court was over for the day. All that was left for Wayne Lonergan was the silver tongue of Edward V. Broderick in his summation on the morrow.

Chapter Nine

THURSDAY, MARCH 30, was a cloudy day in the city of New York. Across the ocean there was tragedy and agony on the Anzio beachhead in Italy as German dive bombers, using fire bombs, turned an American hospital area into a shambles. In London the House of Commons gave Winston Churchill its eighth vote of confidence in four years. In General Sessions in downtown Manhattan the jury seated itself and Judge Wallace ordered the court-room doors locked—the first time in the memory of many that such action had been taken. The doors were locked on everyone, including newsmen.

It was a tense, serious Broderick that began his summa-tion. At the outset he was restrained, but in a matter of minutes his stout face had grown an angry red, the sweat was pouring down his cheeks, and his voice roared into every corner of the courtroom. It was a summation in the old Shakespearean style.

He took up the points of the prosecution's case one by one. There was, for example, the matter of the murder-room candlesticks. "Could you *possibly,* with the short grasp upon the candle holder itself, hit anybody a blow on the head that would cause that candlestick base to take the shape that it is now in? Isn't that distorted shape the result of pressure, such as stamping on it, or throwing it down and stamping on it, rather than from coming in contact with the human skull?" he asked rhetorically.

"There wasn't a single drop of blood upon those candle-sticks or any part of them. And if there was, you would have testimony on it. If there was, it would be in the con-fession.

"I say to you that—general probabilities—these candle-sticks were placed in that room on that bed and under that bed after Mrs. Lonergan had stopped bleeding—and whether they came from the shop of the antique dealer

121

with his one-room, hole-in-the-wall place next to the coffeepot on Lexington Avenue or not, I don't know."

Broderick rambled. He was in full cry, and he darted
from one point to another, the points not necessarily re-
lated.

"You will hear a whole lot, when Mr. Grumet gets up,"
he barked, "about me drawing a red herring over the case,
about me putting the administration of justice on trial.

"That would be the proudest act of my legal career if
I could put the administration of justice, as administered
by Hogan, by Grumet, and by Loehr in this case, on trial
in the public interest."

He returned to the question of the murder itself.

"Assuming Lonergan was there—assume he hit her with
one of those candlesticks. She got up. She yelled. She
shouted. She struggled. Not only after the first blow, but
after the *second* blow. You could not have had much of a
blow in the head while you climb out of bed and begin to
struggle. You certainly were not knocked unconscious. Certainly your awareness was there. She did that not only after
one blow, but after two blows—and she is shouting and
hollering and that goes on for minutes."

Having hardly begun on that aspect, he switched suddenly to Grumet's omission to call Sylvia French to the
stand. "Why didn't he have somebody from the biggest toy
store in the world, Schwartz's, to say that the toy was
bought or was not bought, and have Miss French say there
was a toy there, or there wasn't a toy, and get the picture?"
he shouted.

He was marching up and down before the jury box now,
waving his arms, pleading, denouncing, stopping occasionally to mop his flushed face.

There was only one small change in the appearance of
Wayne Lonergan as he watched his counsel storming
around. He was as imperturbable as ever, but, still chalk-
white, still wearing his blue suit, he sat up straight for virtually the first time.

"No!" Broderick went on fiercely. "There is something
with a stench in that part of the case, too, and that is why
they don't bring them out.

"If Grumet wants you to turn the switch on Lonergan, he should deal openly and frankly with you. You would insist on him doing it if you were buying a house from him, or renting an apartment from him, or selling him an overcoat, or anything else. Why shouldn't he do it when he asks you to go along with your conscience for the rest of your life on the question of whether or not you did justice when you did what you did to Lonergan?"

He came to the testimony of Annalise Schonberg, the nurse. "Now," he said with heavy sarcasm, "the maid upstairs . . . bright, bright as a whip, shrewd and clever.

"Notice how she struggled with the time? Now she is up there. She walks down one flight of stairs and the screaming is still going on right alongside of her. She walks down another flight of stairs. The screaming is still going on. You can hear her down there through the closed door.

"She opens the door, takes in the paper. She walks up the second flight of stairs. She can still hear the screaming. It must have been agonizing screams"—disgust was written on Broderick's face—"when she does not knock. She goes upstairs, does not bring the papers to the little boy on the fourth floor who sent for them, goes into her bedroom directly over Mrs. Lonergan's bedroom, and reads the papers. She finishes a page and a half of the funnies, and then she hears these two piercing screams again."

His sarcasm was biting. A moron or an imbecile "or a calloused person," he continued, might not do anything under those circumstances, "but here is a nurse medically trained. Her obligation is to help preserve, not destroy, life, and she makes no inquiry—does not go down. She does not go down to see if somebody is badly hurt through a chandelier falling down, or a piece of the ceiling, or being burned by some electrical machinery in the home. She has a telephone alongside of her and does not telephone to the police or anybody else. There is something strange about that story—something very strange."

At this point—it was around eleven-five A.M.—Judge Wallace suggested a recess. Broderick, sweating profusely, said he wanted to continue.

"All right, go ahead," the Judge answered.

Still rambling, the defense attorney turned his guns on Ruth Forster, the florist's daughter, who testified she had seen Lonergan leaving Harjes' apartment, dragging his duffel bag and heading for the East River. It was, he said savagely, a "cock-and-bull" tale. "She was a friend of Harjes. Harjes had a lawyer. Why did he have a lawyer? Lonergan couldn't afford a lawyer," Broderick said cryptically.

The scratches on his client's face came next. "Now, they [the Harjes butler and maid] served him breakfast there, and he talked to the maid, and she served him beer after breakfast," he said. "If the scratches were on his face at that time, they would have seen them. Where is Harjes' butler and where is Harjes' maid, both of whom are still working for him up there? Why don't they call them?

"Now, Mrs. Jaburg—a theatrical girl, an ex-show girl, with full knowledge of make-up and its possibilities—she was with Lonergan for the whole of the afternoon. She did not see any scratches on him."

He faced the jury in almost a pleading manner. "I am going to ask you to make this test," he said. "Bring it [the make-up box] into the jury room with you and take a handkerchief; let one of your members volunteer and put it on the scratches on your faces, put it on any part of your body and see what happens. Instead of hiding the scratches, it would emphasize the scratches."

He looked over at Lonergan. "Look at the skin of that boy there," he said, "or look at the color of the skin of any member of the jury. And take some of this and rub it around there—and instead of hiding the scratches, it emphasizes the scratches."

He called for the gray clothes of Harjes' that Lonergan wore on his return to Canada after the murder week end. "These are the clothes that Lonergan was wearing," he said solemnly to the jurors. "Take them into the jury room and examine them." He did not elaborate on this statement.

"Now, the ham and eggs in the bureau drawer," he continued. "Is there anything dark about those, gentlemen? You can take *them* in with you.

"It could be assigned to a drunken man's act. Here is a man that unquestionably was drinking until four or half past four in the morning—cockeyed, no question about that —on leave and enjoying it, and out with a show girl, and hitting the high spots, and drinking." Broderick permitted himself a faint grin.

"I have taken many a drink myself," he said, "but I don't ever remember putting ham and eggs in a bureau. I have done so many funny things that I couldn't understand myself, after, that occurred to me as a drunken man's act." Then he paused and added solemnly. "Not that I say it was."

Next came John Harjes' missing dumbbell. "I don't think Harjes looked at his dumbbell in twenty years—that is not his life," the lawyer barked. "When you stay out like he stays out, meeting people he meets, and going places with people where he goes, you are not interested in any gymnasium."

He turned to Marine Captain Pete Elser. "He doesn't show up in a Marine captain's uniform," he said. "As far as him being a soldier today, he didn't look any different than the young man who sits at my counsel table—a flyer who crashed in this war and wears civilian clothes here during the trial . . . the little lad.

"I say to you," Broderick said scathingly, in the direction of first the Judge and then the jury, "that there is some reason—not an honorable reason, not a creditable reason—why he is here on public exhibition in time of war without his uniform. I asked him why he didn't have it, and he said he didn't know, but headquarters knew and wouldn't tell." He shook his head disgustedly. "Maybe they will tell him right after this case is over."

He turned to Elser's removing of the bedroom door. "And then," he said, "we have the key dropping on the floor, and when I heard that Elser was down in the basement telephoning to his father, Max Elser, I was wondering whether he was telephoning to his father to get the money down there fast—to get it on the line, to get the key to that door back, not the key that was knocked down on the floor, but the key that he or somebody else had in connection with the bedroom. That fact entered my mind because—where is the key? Where is that key?

"Now, what became of it? Did Max Elser buy it back?"

He spoke of Elser's discussion at El Morocco with Gabellini. "They haven't ruled out the possibility that as a result of that resentment upon the part of Gabellini," he declared, "when he got her home, he did give her a little bit of a choking around the throat—not enough to kill her, because the medical testimony doesn't show it was enough to kill her.

"They try to talk about bleeding to death. And she is drunk, she ranges upstairs, she falls against the radiator or falls against the sharp edge of the bed—she does anything, as a drunken person sometimes does, but she is too drunk to take care of herself and she bleeds to death. Does that make murder for anybody?"

There was, he went on, "a conflict between these two men," characterizing Gabellini as "the gigolo, bringing in his fellow python [presumably he meant the Italian word *paisan*] into the coffeepot to talk to him. Whether he brought him into the coffeepot or took him on home to the hole-in-the-wall upstairs, which was a trap for women, the gigolo type, preying on the women—there he was," Broderick said with a flourish, as newsmen tried desperately to parse his sentences.

"He only met Mrs. Lonergan twice before the fatal day —once at a British Empire affair of some kind, and then later for the second time at a Christmas party in 1942," Broderick raged on. "That is his direct testimony. It is there—bring it in.

"Then I began to crossexamine him. Oh, he met her here, he met her there—and he had been over to her home at least ten times. The man was lying right along! There wasn't any question about that!"

Then, almost tenderly, the florid defense lawyer painted a picture of Wayne and Patsy as "two young kids getting along as lots of young kids do get along, both those without a dime and those with millions. Weren't those kids having their fights, the same as any other young kids in the marital status?" he said. "Not a single threat—nobody to call in to say that he ever threatened her. No fight about any will. No testimony from the maids or anybody around the house or anyplace else that there was any quarrel or dissatisfaction. In fact, he was out ten days before with her and Gabellini at the Colony Club and various other places. No indication of resentment."

He paused, then pointed dramatically to Lonergan, still sheet-white, still masklike of face. "A carefree simple country lad that came down here, according to the Canadian confession, and met an old rounder, old Bernheimer-Burton!" he shouted.

"It could happen to anybody—fascinated by the glamour and glitter, the transposition from this small town up there to the international glorification of wine, women, and song here along the pathway.

"They were out together, they went home together—but what have we got? We have got the competition of the twenty-five-year-old boy from Canada against the sophistication and the slipperiness and *savoir faire* of Gabellini, the man from Italy with all the training and all the trickery that comes to masterminds who prey on women. Young Lonergan couldn't meet that competition—he wouldn't recognize that competition. Gabellini is too subtle. Gabellini could convince this lad he was the greatest friend in the world. He was just trying to see those two young kids get along. Gabellini—who was old enough to be Lonergan's father."

Broderick's speech went on—furious, explosive, at times incoherent, but strangely compelling. It was ham acting of the worst kind, and yet there was a kind of primitive urgency about it.

"Here," he declaimed, "was a Canadian boy, and he was here in this situation, and there came the time when he went up and signed up with his native colors as a flier.

"He was facing death at all times—didn't have to be over in a combat zone to be facing death; the training course itself carried many of them down to death and serious injury. He wasn't caring much about the Bernheimer millions then. As he said to his doctor, 'I may only last ten days—what difference does it make?' The same carefree lad!"

Broderick paused. Then, he continued, he would be happy if, in the years to come, Wayne Lonergan, Jr., reading his obituary, could turn to his father and say, "Dad, is that the lawyer who fought intrinsic wealth, who fought intrinsic official arrogance, and fought every obstacle in his way to see that justice was done to you?"

Broderick came at last to the question of the taking down of the "confession, so called." His sarcasm was at its heaviest. He directed the jurors to study the confession, and to note that Lonergan was asked, during it, "Will you have a drink?" Not "Do you want a glass of water?" or "Do you want time out?"

"And I say what was happening there," the lawyer thundered, "is that he was drinking neat, all the time he was making the confession! Liquor permeates the entire thing, all the way through.

"Gentlemen, that is the thing that nails down the testimony in the confession: 'Will you have a drink?' He was not only drunk when he was brought into the district attorney's office; he was kept drunk by this confession and he was kept drunk only to a certain standard. Mahoney sent out different times during the night to get a lot of black coffee. What was happening? The fatigue and the liquor was wearing him out; his awareness was passing, was becoming weakened, and Mahoney was sending out for coffee to sober him sufficiently so they could still continue."

He had been talking for two hours. Now, nearing the end, Broderick stormed up and down in front of the jury box. "Gentlemen," he exclaimed, "it is a terrible indictment, and I say to you that when this case is over, four men should be in state's prison—District Attorney Hogan, Assistant District Attorney Grumet, Assistant District Attorney Loehr, who perjured himself here, and Captain Mahoney!"

He stopped, sweating and panting. Then he took a breath and leaned over the rail of the jury box. In a low, conversational tone, he said:

"Now, gentlemen, there comes the time when I must

make a transfer. I am at the end of my relationship to the presentation of evidence and summation in this case. I am now transferring from my hands and my conscience and to your hands and to your conscience a Canadian soldier, a Canadian father.

"I trust that you will handle that as I know you will— an American gentleman desiring to see that justice be done."

For a moment the courtroom was still. Those that sat there looked from the worn-out, emotionally drained Broderick to Wayne Lonergan, who had yet to say an audible word in that room. He was expressionless.

Then Judge Wallace called for a brief recess. It was of only minutes' duration. When it was over, Jacob Grumet, lean, dour, businesslike, rose to sum up for the presecution.

"During the course of his summing up to you gentlemen this morning," Grumet began, "Mr. Broderick attacked every witness in the case—including the District Attorney, Mr. Hogan, Mr. Loehr, myself, and, I might add, all the members of the New York Police Department who were engaged in the investigation of this case. I do not intend, during the course of my remarks to you, to defend any of these people. I do not believe they need any defense at my hands."

The brisk young assistant district attroney said he wouldn't engage in any "vituperation or abuse," but rather would content himself with summarizing and reviewing the evidence. He pointed out how important it was for the jurors to maintain a judicial attitude of mind, "one that is not moved by any prejudice nor moved by any sympathy."

He reminded the jurymen that he had asked them at the outset to note that the District Attorney had only Lonergan's statement as to what happened in the bedroom "immediately prior to the killing." This brought Broderick to his feet, protesting that "there isn't a single thing in the confession wherein the defendant said he murdered her," but Judge Wallace overruled the objection.

"Gentlemen," Grumet said, "this is murder, and nothing else, and I will show you that it is."

He then referred to Lonergan's claim to have argued with Patsy over her conduct. "Do you really believe that?" the prosecutor asked. "Do you believe that this man, who admitted he was unfaithful, who was running around with other women, and who only a few hours before had been out with another woman, killed her for that reason?"

Grumet mentioned Lonergan's Sunday date for lunch with Jean Murphy Jaburg at the Plaza Hotel. "Did you ever hear anything in your life more cold-blooded than that?" he demanded. "Is that the act of a man who says that he was concerned about his wife, who was separated from him and, as a matter of fact, had to get rid of him because of misbehavior?

"He was not concerned about that. His marriage to this deceased had enabled him to live in the lap of luxury. Work was entirely foreign to his nature. Think of this man being married for a period of two years and not even thinking of doing a stitch of work. Then he is cut off from his source of income.

"I tell you that he was very much interested in that money. He now realized that all was over. It rankled. He resented it. You must remember the type that he is—just a parasite."

The lawyer, describing Lonergan as "very shrewd, particularly where his own interests are concerned," spoke of the eleven hours or so that lapsed before Patsy's body was found. During that time, he charged, Lonergan was "busily engaged covering up his acts, so far as he possibly could—removing and destroying any and all evidence that might point to him as the perpetrator of this crime and, after he gets through with all that dirty business, leaves the jurisdiction . . . placing himself outside of the reach of the authorities here."

Grumet then accused Lonergan of "lies and lies and lies." He referred to Broderick's claim that the uniform could not have been thrown into the East River from the spot where it was supposed to have been tossed, "but did he tell you what happened to the uniform? He was strangely and significantly silent on that subject."

He recalled the note Lonergan left for Harjes. "Lies and

lies," he said scathingly. "He was asked how he had gotten
the scratches which were on his face, and he stated there
that he got those in an encounter with this strange soldier,
while they were engaged in some acts of degeneracy. He
was willing to stoop to the lowest depths to avoid telling
the truth.

"We knew Lonergan was lying!" Grumet exclaimed
sharply. "We knew that story didn't have the ring of truth.
By then we were convinced that he was the murderer."

The prosecutor took up Lonergan's statement that he
was at Patsy's apartment for from three quarters of an
hour to an hour, which would place the killing somewhere
around nine-thirty A.M. Sunday. "Now I say to you,"
Grumet added, "that he murdered his wife very soon after
he got to her apartment—that there could not have been
any long discussion." He pointed out how Annalise Schonberg, the nurse, had said she thought she had heard the
screams about eight-fifty-five A.M.

"I say to you," Grumet went on, "that this defendant
went to this apartment with the idea of murdering his wife,
and he murdered her within a matter of a few minutes
after he got there."

As for the fact that the confession was not signed, "Gentlemen," Grumet said, "that is just so much nonsense." It
was common practice, he declared, to take statements from
suspects stenographically and present them "just as Lonergan's confession was presented here."

Apparently grimly determined to prove premeditation,
Grumet said flatly that "this was a brutal, cold-blooded,
deliberate crime." He said Lonergan had walked from the
bed to the table to pick up the first candlestick—a distance, he added, of some seventeen feet. Broderick arose to
dispute the distance. Judge Wallace told him to sit down.

After hitting Patsy with the candlestick, Grumet said,
Lonergan walked back and got the second candlestick,
"covering another distance of thirty-four feet." Then, he
said, Patsy, after being hit for the second time, dragged
herself to the other side of the bed, "but he was determined to kill her, and he went around the bed and the
settee and grabbed hold of her as she was standing.

"She didn't stand a chance," he declared. "And he grabbed her by the throat, with both hands, and continued to strangle—he says for three minutes." He looked at the jurors. "If you want any idea of what three minutes are," he said, "when you get back to your jury room you can take your watches out and determine for yourselves."

He rocked back on his heels.

"Gentlemen," he said, "can there be any question but that this was just as I have described it—cold-blooded and deliberate murder? Could he have plenty of opportunity during all of that time to reflect and consider what he was doing—whether he should kill or not kill—and to formulate a very definite purpose to kill?"

Grumet then told the jurors that they would be instructed by the Judge about what constituted murder in the first degree, "but let me say this: In my opinion, the killing of Patricia Lonergan by this defendant was from a deliberate and premeditated design to accomplish her death, and is murder in the first degree." The law does not require, he noted, that premeditation "shall exist for any great length of time before the crime is committed."

Then, coming to the finish of his brief summation—it took only forty-seven minutes—Grumet reviewed Lonergan's actions as recounted in the confession, and commented bitingly about the defendant's having called Jean Jaburg at eleven A.M. Sunday, less than two hours after the brutal slaying. "So that, even before he finished the dirty job of getting rid of his bloody uniform—perhaps even while he was still engaged in cutting it up and stuffing it into the duffel bag in Harjes' apartment—he was already on the phone trying to date up Jean Murphy Jaburg for lunch," he said with obvious disgust, "and with his wife's battered body lying alone in the bedroom at Three-thirteen East Fifty-first Street, murdered by him, he very calmly sat in the Oak Room of the Plaza, having lunch with Jean Jaburg."

Grumet stopped for a moment, then looked squarely at the jurors.

"I know, gentlemen, that you are going to make an honest and intelligent effort to find a verdict which is based strictly on the evidence, and on the law as it will be given to you by the court, without any prejudice and without any sympathy," he said.

"Decide this case on the facts—and based on those facts and based on the truth, in behalf of the people of the State of New York, I ask you to find this defendant guilty of murder in its first degree."

Grumet sat down. The jury leaned back. Judge Wallace made his customary "Do not discuss this case" talk to the panel, and court was over for Thursday, March 30, 1944.

After the adjournment, Broderick spoke briefly to Lonergan in an anteroom. Then he left the building, pausing just long enough to tell newsmen that "the defendant feels confident as to the outcome of the trial, and we are satisfied with all that has gone on up to this point."

Chapter Ten

A MERE HANDFUL of spectators was in General Sessions on Friday morning. Judge Wallace entered the room shortly after eleven o'clock, and promptly ordered the doors locked. A sign was hung on the outside of the doors, "No admittance. Judge charging jury."

Wayne Lonergan, seated at the defense table, was flanked as usual by Edward Broderick, Broderick's brother Joe, and attorneys William Merritt and S. Bertram Friedman. Loehr and another assistant district attorney, Vincent J. Dermody, sat with Grumet. At precisely eleven-eighteen the Judge began to speak in a firm, clear voice.

In a way, it was a model of a judge's charge. Carefully Wallace reviewed the facts. Emphatically he warned the jurors that they were "the sole and exclusive judges of the facts." Painstakingly he reminded them that they could bring in one of five verdicts.

It seemed obvious that the Judge, if not the jury, didn't believe the crime was premeditated. The state, he told the jurors, had produced no evidence to show that Lonergan "made up his mind to kill" his heiress wife on that cold Sunday. "No burden is on any defendant to prove he is innocent," the Judge said. Then he took up the phrase "reasonable doubt." While the people are not expected to establish anything on a mathematical basis, he said, such a doubt couldn't be decided "on a whim, a surmise, or a caprice. It's an honest doubt, based on the evidence," he added.

Nor had any evidence been introduced to prove that the defendant was mentally unbalanced, either through inheritance or from any other cause, Judge Wallace continued.

He returned to the question of premeditation. In considering the degrees of guilt, he cautioned the jury, "you must be satisfied the killing was accompanied by intent on the part of the defendant to accomplish the killing of Pa-

134

tricia Lonergan. Intent is a mental operation," he noted, "and it is difficult to prove what is inside a person's mind. A person who plans to kill another does not notify photographers."

It was the confession, he said at last, that was the important item in this trial. The question pertaining to it was "whether the defendant made his statement voluntarily. If you believe that it was a voluntary confession," he added, "and that additional proof of the crime charged has been submitted, then you have the right to find the defendant guilty. If there is a reasonable doubt, you must acquit him."

There was, Judge Wallace went on, no evidence whatever that Lonergan was plied with liquor to get that statement. "The evidence is to the contrary," he said.

He reminded the jurors that they were entitled to disregard or accept all or any part of a witness' testimony, if it felt such testimony was not the truth. "When any inconsistencies appear," he advised, "if they do, your duty is to reconcile them."

He pointed out one discrepancy in Lonergan's confession when compared with Jean Jaburg's testimony. Lonergan had said he took her to Harjes' apartment before returning her to her own place. She had testified that they went directly to her own apartment after leaving the Blue Angel.

All during the Judge's charge, the jury watched him closely. Occasionally a juror would glance over at the defendant. At twelve-twenty-eight the charge was finished in the strangely subdued courtroom. The jury filed into its own spacious room at twelve-forty-six, intending first to eat luncheon, and then to get down to the matter of Wayne Lonergan's guilt or innocence. Attendants, meanwhile, took Lonergan to a detention cell on the thirteenth floor of the court building, where he had tomato rice soup and bread for lunch.

Newsmen, meanwhile, found grist for their mill elsewhere. In the corridor, after the jury had received the case, they cornered Owen M. Voight, a chemical manufacturer who had been one of two alternates on the jury. When they asked him for his personal opinion, he said he thought Lonergan was guilty of not less than murder in the second degree.

A thickset, medium-sized man, with graying hair and an easy, slow smile, Voight admitted the possibility of premeditation, and he said that if he were voting and the others had found a conviction of murder in the first degree, he probably would have gone along with it. He gave his opinion, incidentally, only after the judge had discharged him from further participation in the trial, and he had nothing more to do with the case.

Voight spoke of Broderick. The defense counsel's summation, he said, was "pitiful." "He did not convince me of anything and he didn't disprove anything the state had built up," the alternate declared.

As for premeditation: "Yes, there was premeditation, but I'm not so sure it was strong enough to warrant murder in the first degree. After all, what did it amount to but a fight between a man and his wife? He was jealous of the men she was going out with." As for the attempted purchase of arsenic, Voight said he thought that was part of the premeditation. "I think he wanted to kill his wife to get hold of the money," he added.

Of Lonergan, Voight said, "I think he was just a mercenary fellow who wanted to live a life of ease. I feel sorry for him." He reflected for a moment; then he shook his head. "But I wouldn't vote for anything less than murder in the second degree."

The newsmen asked him what he thought of Patsy Lonergan. He avoided the question first, saying he never spoke about a woman he didn't know. But when they asked him if he felt she was a butterfly, he said she wasn't. "She was just a woman who liked to have a Scotch and soda and put a nickel in the jukebox and dance. She was an ordinary woman who was able to pay her way wherever she wanted to go."

It was just another Friday afternoon in New York; the day dragged on and a light, misty rain began to fall. It was much like that other day in the October just past, the

events of which had brought all these people to this courtroom in downtown Manhattan.

At six-fifty, the first hint came. The jury filed back into
the courtroom to ask Judge Wallace to repeat his comments about the various degrees of homicide and the pen-
alties they carried. The newsmen's ears pricked up. When
the judge had finished carefully outlining the degrees, they
broke for the bank of eight public telephones in the corridor outside—to discover, with anguished howls, that all
eight were out of order. A direct wire to a news service
had been set up; that, too, was out of order.

For a few moments it looked as if an intramural war
would begin, with reporters yelling charges at one another.
However, there were a couple of New York Telephone
Company detectives on hand, and they suddenly saw a
fourteen-year-old boy slip a device for an earphone into
his pocket. The police picked him up, and he told them
that he worked for a radio station, and had been told to
remove the devices from the phones so that the station
could score a news beat. The devices were put back, the
boy was released, and the newsmen returned, with sighs, to
sitting out the death watch.

At ten-twenty-three P.M., the Lonergan jury filed back
into Part 9, General Sessions. William Byrne, the foreman,
arose and turned to look at the defendant. Lonergan sat
there, still and calm, looking more boyish than ever. When
Byrne spoke, his voice was quiet but firm:

"We, the jurors, find the defendant, Wayne Lonergan,
guilty of murder in the second degree."

For a second, Wayne Lonergan sat there without change.
Then, slowly, he bowed his head and bit his lip. Some
people thought they heard him sob.

Broderick demanded that the jurors be polled, and they
were. Court Clerk Arnold Sayre inquired of each, "Is that
your verdict?" Each replied yes, clearly and distinctly, as
the defendant seemed to be struggling to control his emo-
tions.

Judge Wallace then dismissed the jury, and there was
one last detail to attend to—the formality of conveying
Lonergan's pedigree to the court clerk. It was the first

time his voice had been heard in the courtroom, and it was weak and strained as he said he was twenty-six, his address was the University of Texas (where he had trained with the RCAF), he was a Roman Catholic and a moderate drinker. The clerk's last question was: "Are you married?"

You hardly could hear the low, hesitant "Yes."

Court was over.

Lonergan was returned to his cell in the Tombs; he fell almost immediately into an exhausted sleep, after the guards had taken the usual precaution of removing his tie, belt, and shoelaces, although Commissioner of Correction Amoroso felt there was little probability that his "model" prisoner would try to kill himself.

Edward Broderick gathered his papers together, refused to comment on the verdict, and left quickly. Joe Broderick lingered a little while and told reporters, "Lonergan is a soldier of fortune. It's his belief that if his number is up, it's up."

District Attorney Hogan complimented Grumet and Loehr. Grumet, although he had demanded the first-degree conviction, said the verdict was "fair and intelligent."

Wayne Lonergan was brought back to General Sessions on Monday, April 17, 1944, a day when spring was definitely in the New York air.

In the two-week interval, he had been so quiet a prisoner at the Tombs that an official at the prison said, "We don't even know he's here." Before court began, Broderick told newsmen that Lonergan wasn't depressed by the prospect of imprisonment, and even had been discussing legal moves to obtain custody of little Billy. It also was learned that Wayne's last statement to the court's probation officers, taken after his conviction on March 21, had been a bitter denial of his guilt.

"I don't know who killed my wife," he swore, "but I didn't."

The sentencing was swift. Lonergan entered the court at ten-thirty A.M. He was hoping for the customary minimum for second-degree murder, twenty years to life. With good behavior, that would see him out of prison in thirteen years, still a man in his thirties.

He strode into the courtroom as impassively as ever, dressed in the same blue suit. He nodded to Broderick, but otherwise glanced neither left nor right. The clerk of the court called off his name, and Lonergan stood and faced Judge Wallace.

The Judge picked up the probation report, glanced at it momentarily, and then looked down at Lonergan. "You are sentenced to from thirty-five years to life," he said.

The sentence sank in slowly, as the conviction had. Lonergan first gazed ahead stonily; then his eyes widened, his face paled, his eyes flickered. He turned and looked at Broderick. Their eyes met, and then the prisoner, with his escort of guards, walked out of court, on his way to Sing Sing Prison.

Later, Broderick said he would appeal, and still later it was reported that Lonergan, stung by the heavy sentence, had raged and charged he had been "double-crossed" by the District Attorney and railroaded to prison.

On April 21, 1944, Judge John G. Freschi, before whom the Lonergan trial had begun, convicted Edward V. Broderick of four counts of contempt of court and sentenced the lawyer to a fine of $250 and thirty days in jail on each count, the terms to run concurrently. Later the sentence was modified to the fine only. Freschi said he had witnessed on March 3 "a most violent, vociferous outburst of unjustifiable and irrelevant vituperation, insinuation, abuse, false statements, shouting, table pounding, and an address to the audience lacking self-control and other conduct unbecoming a lawyer in the defense of his client." He said he never had seen and, "indeed, never heard of, conduct so unprofessional."

Broderick said in his behalf only that he was "under a prolonged mental strain, the like of which I never want to experience again. A less stable person would have succombed to the stress," he added.

Still later, a Brooklyn Law School professor of medical and legal jurisprudence, George I. Swetlow, sued Broderick for one thousand dollars for services in connection with the defense. Broderick admitted consulting with Swetlow, but said the professor had proposed a line of defense he regarded as "ridiculous." Swetlow said he had asked Broderick how he had planned to defend Lonergan, and "he said that he was like a wrestler waiting to catch a hold—that the trial was to him a catch-as-catch-can matter, and that he was hoping that he would catch a defense as the case proceeded."

Still later, the New York State Bar Association's committee on professional ethics drew up a scathing report on Broderick's conduct, and, finally, three years after the Lonergan case, the same Judge Wallace fined Broderick one hundred dollars and five days in jail for contempt—"studied insolence and defiance"—in connection with the defense of a patrolman who strangled a woman.

Six years after Wayne Lonergan went to prison, Mario Gabellini came into the news again. The story was brief. In the East 60th Street apartment of Gabellini—"who has an eerie faculty for associating with women on the verge of their melancholy departure from this world," as the *New York Journal-American* put it—a pretty, red-haired showgirl named Patricia Stousland took poison. She died an hour later in Bellevue Hospital. Gabellini was out of the apartment at the time. When he returned, he said he had known the girl for ten years and was "entirely mystified" by her act.

There was one final loose end of the Lonergan case.

On February 5, 1954, not quite ten years after the sensational trial, an eleven-year-old boy who had thought himself an orphan was confronted with what one newspaper called "a staggering set of discoveries."

The boy's name was William Anthony Burton—but it had been, until it was legally changed, Wayne William Lonergan.

Billy Lonergan was given into the legal guardianship of his grandmother, Lucille Wolfe Burton, after the trial ended, and he had lived quietly with her in Manhattan. His name was changed in 1947, four years after the murder. He was led to believe that both his parents were dead.

On January 25 of 1954, however, Stella S. Housman, Billy's eighty-five-year-old great-grandmother, died at Palm Beach. Eleven dàys later, her will was filed for probate, and William Anthony Burton learned from Lucille Burton for the first time that his mother had been murdered in one of Manhattan's most spectacular slayings, that his father was not dead, but instead was still in prison for the murder, and that he had just inherited more than $6,800,-000, the estimated value of what Broderick used to call so bitterly the Burton-Bernheimer millions.

Mrs. Housman left Billy $5,000 "as a memento of me," but the bulk of his fortune came from the trust fund established by Stella's first husband, Max Bernheimer. The boy became sole heir.

There seemed little hope that Billy's father would share in the estate. His conviction cost him his civil rights, and even should Billy die before reaching twenty-one, Wayne's only chance would be through winning a pardon that restored those rights. "He could come into some of that money," legal experts said, "only as a gift from his son, or in case his son should designate him as heir."

THE END